UNCLE MILTON'S HOUSE

A Novel

J.J. Mott

Burin Books

To Lizzy

CONTENTS

OCTOBER 29, 1983

Simeon Kulak walked out with the others when the party began to break up. It had been a good night, except for that one embarrassing moment, but even that hadn't been so bad. Brenda Gilmartin, dressed as an Indian squaw, touched his arm as she wished him goodnight, and Simeon felt his cheeks grow warm.

"Thank you for coming, Simeon," she said. "I hope you had a good time."

"Oh yes," Simeon returned. "Good time." Simeon shook his head and blinked hard. "I mean, I had a good time. A very good time. Thank you."

Brenda smiled. "I'm glad. Be careful driving home, now."

"Oh, I will," Simeon said, shooting a glance at his prized possession parked on the street. Mark Mason appeared in the doorway, and Simeon stepped off the porch to make room for the high school quarterback.

"Later, Brenda," Mark said, his broad shoulder pads brushing both sides of the doorframe as he stepped out.

Brenda turned to face Mark and the other two football players who followed behind him, all dressed in the same unoriginal costumes. Taking that as his cue to leave, Simeon started walking toward his car, having run out of things to say anyway. He strolled down the driveway, feeling pretty good about himself. Brenda's Halloween party was the first social event he had attended since Bobby Silverman's thirteenth birthday party five years earlier, and Simeon thought it had gone well. He had been called by the nickname he so deeply despised only once during the night, but then Alison Kowalski yelled at Flash for saying it. Brenda said something as well, and although he didn't really like that kind of attention, it made Simeon feel good inside. He was used to teachers and other adults standing up for him, but not his classmates. Mark Mason even said something to Flash, but Simeon hadn't heard what it was because Brenda was talking to him.

"Never mind him, Simeon," she said. "He's just being a bully." Then Brenda asked if he liked the pumpkin-shaped cookie he was holding, but since he hadn't tried it yet, he took a bite. The cookie was very good, and he wanted to tell her so, but Brenda turned and followed Flash out of the garage before he was done chewing. Things settled down again after that, and several of Simeon's classmates talked to him, mostly about his car, as if he were no different than anyone else. He didn't think he had ever talked so much in all his life, but it was a good feeling. Other kids seldom spoke to him, and he knew it was because he wasn't as smart as they were. Simeon's mother believed it was better for him to attend a school where his classmates were a bit smarter rather than go to a special school where it was the other way around. He just needed to be patient and do his best, and it seemed like his patience was finally paying off.

The firethorn-red Nova gleamed under the glow of the streetlamp, and Simeon beamed with pride as he opened the driver's side door. He took great care of the car, and it showed. He washed and buffed it every Saturday, as long as it wasn't raining, and applied so much Armor All to the interior that you would slide across the vinyl seats on turns if you weren't buckled in. Simeon got behind the wheel and grinned as the V-8 engine roared to life. David Higgins, dressed as a Viking, gave him a thumbs-up as he passed in front of the headlights. Simeon grinned and returned the gesture before pulling away from the curb.

Despite the Nova's power, Simeon always drove slowly and carefully, obeying all traffic laws. He took his driving responsibilities very seriously. He drove past houses decorated with grinning jack-o'-lanterns on their front steps and the occasional home displaying genuinely frightening props in their yards. Simeon didn't like those houses. Although it didn't bother him as much as it once had, Halloween was a holiday he had feared since childhood. He once sneaked out of his room after bedtime and secretly watched a horror movie his parents had on TV from behind the sofa in the living room. It showed people turning into monsters with mouths full of pointed teeth, and it frightened Simeon so much that he started crying and gave himself away. His parents allowed him to keep his bedroom door open and the hallway light on that night, but he still woke up screaming from a nightmare. He continued to have nightmares for the whole week leading up to Halloween and believed that the spooky holiday was somehow responsible. In the days leading up to Brenda Gilmartin's party, he grew anxious, worried that there might be some truly frightening costumes, but it wasn't like that at all. Reggie Thomas was the only person to come as a monster, but he wasn't scary at all, and he kept the plastic vampire fangs out of his mouth for most of the night. Still, Simeon couldn't shake the childhood fears that the holiday stirred up as he drove on, and it only worsened when the residential neighborhood gave way to dense woods.

Fabers Road wound through the hilly woods that separated North Coddington—the rich side of town, where everyone had large homes and sprawling lawns —from South, where the houses were closely packed together on small lots. Driving on that stretch of road at night always made Simeon uneasy, but it was even worse with thoughts of Halloween and monster movies haunting his mind. He switched on the radio, looking for a distraction. "Abracadabra" by The Steve Miller Band was playing, and Simeon was just starting to relax when he thought he heard a groaning sound.

Had that come through the speakers? he wondered.

The music played on, but Simeon didn't hear anything beyond the familiar lyrics. He glanced in the rearview mirror and saw the dark road unwinding behind him. The sound seemed to have come from somewhere close, but he couldn't be sure. He turned down the radio volume and held his breath, listening for the sound to come again.

It did.

And this time, it sounded like a growl.

Simeon stepped on the gas, causing the car to accelerate along with his heart rate. He wanted to be out of the woods and under the bright streetlights of South Coddington as quickly as possible.

But the sound had come from inside the car.

Simeon looked in the rearview mirror again, and this time, he saw something.

A monster—an actual monster—sat in the backseat, its hands curled into claws on either side of its head. The monster's face was a brownish-gray, and its skin sagged and jiggled as if it were dripping off. Its eyes were mere slits in the center of the drooping face. The creature roared and reached between the front seats, knocking the armrest down. Simeon shrieked and twisted in his seat to distance himself from the creature. The monster roared again, only this time it sounded like it was trying to say something. The engine also roared, and Simeon realized his foot had pressed the accelerator to the floor as he twisted in his seat. Light streamed through the windshield, and he knew he had reached the edge of the woods where Foreman's Garage and the first streetlight marked the south side of town. The light also touched the monster's face, which immediately ducked down, vanishing behind the seat. Simeon lifted his foot off the gas as he turned around in his seat, but it was too late. The Nova crumpled under Richard Foreman's flatbed truck, the cruel lip of the metal deck slicing through everything.

1

Gordon Nagel pulled into the narrow driveway of his uncle's house and took a long, final drag of his cigarette. The ember consumed the last bit of tobacco, right up to the filter, until he felt the heat on his lips and fingers. He opened the driver's side door to drop the butt on the ground, and the car lurched forward when his foot slipped off the brake. Cursing the column shifter as if it were to blame, he slammed the lever into the park position. The engine continued to sputter and cough after the key was removed from the ignition and persisted until Gordon was out of the car and standing beside it. The old Chevy Caprice had been doing this for some time now, and he suspected the engine would soon take its last gasp.

After removing the two bags of groceries from the back seat, Gordon kicked the door shut with the heel of his work boot. He applied more force than necessary and stumbled awkwardly as the door slammed home, causing something to spill out of one of the bags in his arms. Not wanting to put the bags down, he made his way to the front steps, planning to retrieve the missing item after bringing the groceries inside the house. Sidestepping the aluminum wheelchair ramp, Gordon ascended the three steps to the covered porch landing. He managed to slide the key into the lock without dropping any groceries, but nearly dropped one of the bags as he turned the knob and shouldered the door open. Uncle Milton sat in his wheelchair, three feet from the old television, its bluish light reflected in the lenses of his eyeglasses. He glanced briefly in Gordon's direction before returning his attention to the Final Jeopardy round.

"I got your groceries," Gordon said, nudging the door shut with his elbow.

"Put 'em on the table," Uncle Milton said without taking his eyes off the TV.

Gordon carried the groceries to the kitchen table, where he began removing items. When the game show was over, Uncle Milton would roll into the kitchen and direct the placement of each item. Gordon knew where everything belonged, but his uncle insisted that it be done under his direction.

"What is Kalamazoo?"

Gordon rolled his eyes when he heard his uncle's answer phrased as a question. Uncle Milton always yelled "Kalamazoo" at the TV when he didn't know the clue response. A moment later, he rolled into the kitchen.

"Did you get everything you were supposed to?"

"Yeah, I got everything," Gordon said with more assurance than he felt.

Uncle Milton eyed the items on the table. "Cereal and cookies next to the toaster," he said. "All the canned stuff to the right of the sink."

Gordon did as his uncle directed. He placed everything exactly where he was told to avoid future accusations of putting something in the wrong place.

"Milk and yogurt in the fridge." Uncle Milton scowled at the table before turning the look on Gordon. "Where's the cottage cheese? You were supposed to get cottage cheese."

Gordon scanned the table and looked inside the empty bags. He could have sworn he bought cottage cheese. It was always on the list, and the list rarely changed. "I don't know," he said. "The idiot at the store probably forgot to put it in the bag."

"That's why you should always bag the stuff yourself," Uncle Milton chided. "Why do I always have to tell you that? Now you'll have to go back tomorrow and file a complaint. Where's the receipt?"

Gordon fished the receipt out of one of the bags and pushed it across the table. He leaned against the counter and stared at the kitchen floor while his uncle droned on. The faded linoleum was heavily worn, cracked, and peeling up at the edges. It needed to be replaced, but Uncle Milton was no longer interested in making home improvements. At almost ninety, he was content as long as the plumbing worked and the roof remained intact over his head.

Gordon often thought about the improvements he would make to the house once it became his. Although it had never been formally discussed, Gordon felt sure he would inherit the old house when his uncle died. He had never seen a will, but he assumed one existed. If not, the house should still filter down to him through his mother, since Karen had no use for the place. Gordon's sister was riding high on the hog with her highfalutin husband out in Colorado and had assumed power of attorney over their mother's affairs after her stroke. Their mother now lived in a nursing home, also in Colorado, with Karen footing the bill. Gordon and Uncle Milton still lived in their hometown, and the burden of caring for their mother's brother had fallen on him. When Uncle Milton died, the house should automatically pass through their mother, his next of kin, and then on to Gordon and Karen. The old pile wasn't worth much, so it made sense that his sister would let Gordon have it. She certainly didn't need whatever money they'd get from selling the place. At the very least, Gordon could buy out her share over time. It's not like she'd take him to court if he missed a payment here and there. Gordon had considered the various scenarios many times, and he was confident that the house would eventually be his.

"Are you listening to me, Boy?"

"Yeah, I hear you," Gordon said, hoping he hadn't missed anything important. "I'll go back to the store tomorrow."

Gordon just wanted to go back to the bar, but he was out of money. He didn't have enough to pay for that last shot of whiskey and had promised Mack that he would return with what he owed, along with a generous tip.

"I'm gonna need some money for gas," Gordon said as matter-of-factly as possible. "I nearly ran out on the way over here."

Uncle Milton had already pointed his wheelchair toward the living room, but he swiveled around to shoot a stern glare at Gordon. "Don't you ever have any money of your own, Boy?"

Gordon hated that question as much as he disliked being called "Boy," but he was used to hearing both. He ignored the question and pressed on. "You also need a new rake so I can clean up the yard," he said, pleased with his quick thinking. "The old one broke when I was cleaning up the yard last month." That was a lie, but Gordon knew his uncle had no idea what was in the storage shed anymore. More importantly, it would require him to shell out some extra money. Uncle Milton shook his head and wheeled out of the kitchen toward his bedroom, grumbling all the way.

Gordon followed his uncle partway down the short hall and then turned into the bathroom, which had recently been modified to accommodate a wheelchair. The doorway had been widened, and metal handrails had been installed on the walls to help with transfers from the wheelchair to the toilet or the new walk-in shower tub. After relieving himself, Gordon brought some towels down from a shelf and placed them on top of the wicker hamper beside the sink. When he came out, he found Uncle Milton parked once again in front of the television watching Wheel of Fortune. The sound of chiming bells filled the living room as Vanna White magically illuminated the letter boxes with a touch of her hand.

"I put some towels out for you in case you want to take a shower," Gordon said, scanning the kitchen table for the cash he hoped to find but did not see.

"Make sure you get a decent rake," Uncle Milton said, holding up a check, his eyes never leaving the TV. "Don't buy any cheap Chinese crap."

Gordon's shoulders sagged. He had been hoping for cash. He wanted to return to Cormack's, settle his tab, and have another drink or two, but Uncle Milton had just ruined any chance of that happening because he wouldn't be able to cash the check until tomorrow. He pinched the check from his uncle's hand, glancing at the amount before tucking it into the breast pocket of his denim jacket. Gordon considered the price of a rake and how much of the fifty dollars would be left over for him as he opened the front door.

"There's more than enough there for a rake and gasoline," Uncle Milton opined. "And don't forget to get the cottage cheese!"

"Yeah, I know," Gordon muttered, stepping out into

the cool night air. "I'll see you tomorrow."

As he walked around to the driver's side door of the Chevy, Gordon suddenly slipped when something squashed under his shoe. His foot shot out from under him, and he fell hard on his backside. He mumbled a string of curses as he got back up, brushing wet leaves off the back of his pants. The container responsible for his fall lay crushed on the ground, lumpy white cottage cheese sprayed all over the driveway as if fired from a shotgun.

"Fuck me," Gordon muttered, realizing that he had forgotten to retrieve the item that had fallen out of the grocery bag. "I *knew* I bought it."

Gordon ignored the mess. If the cats that were constantly loitering around the neighbor's house didn't eat it, something would crawl out of the sewers to gobble it up overnight. Gordon had seen rats in the neighborhood more times than he could count. He climbed into the driver's seat and coaxed the Chevy as the engine struggled to turn over. After a few reluctant chugs, the engine roared to life. Gordon backed the car out into the narrow, one-way street and drove off, clipping a garbage can at the corner. He headed for the loft apartment he referred to as "The Dump," wondering all the while if he would find anything to drink at the bottom of one of the bottles there.

2

Gordon approached the counter and presented the check and his driver's license to the teller. The young woman smiled and asked Gordon if he wished to cash the check or transfer the money to another account.

"Cash it," Gordon said after a moment's hesitation. The teller, whom he had dealt with many times, had never asked that question before.

The teller, noticing Gordon's puzzled expression, said, "I only ask because you're both the payer *and* the payee. People sometimes write a check to transfer money from one account to another."

"What do you mean?" Gordon asked, still confused. "My uncle wrote that check."

The teller nodded patiently and held up the check for Gordon to see. She pointed to the top corner where Gordon's name was printed directly below his uncle's. "It's a joint account. You could have made the check out yourself." She slipped the check into the scanner. "Don't worry, it's fine," she said. "Either way works." She slipped two twenties and a ten into an envelope and passed it to Gordon.

"Oh, I get it now," Gordon said, recalling a recent visit to the bank with his sister and uncle. "It's that power of attorney thing we set up a little while ago. I remember them saying they were gonna put my name on the account."

The teller tapped a few keys and read something on the monitor behind the counter. "That's right," she said. "The joint account was opened two weeks ago."

"Yeah," Gordon said, slightly embarrassed. "I guess I forgot."

"No worries. It takes a little while for them to print the checks. Your uncle probably just received them."

Gordon nodded and turned as the teller wished him a nice day, but he was too distracted to offer her the reply she deserved. He recalled signing some documents at the bank two Saturdays ago, but he hadn't completely understood everything that was said and done. He signed several papers earlier that same day at a lawyer's office with his sister and Uncle Milton, then followed up at the bank, where they created a joint account. The legal jargon made little sense to Gordon, and he had not bothered to read any of the documents that were pushed in front of him. He just signed when and where he was told. Karen knew the process was beyond Gordon's understanding and promised to explain everything later, which she did to some extent. She told Gordon that granting him power of attorney would be helpful if, or when, something like Uncle Milton's recent accident happened again. It would enable Gordon to handle any immediate decisions, should the need arise, since he was the only family member still living near their uncle.

"I can't be expected to fly in from Colorado every time something happens here," Karen had said. "Nick and I paid for all the necessary improvements to Uncle Milton's house, so it's only fair that you take care of his day-to-day needs and any immediate situations that come up. You can now make decisions on his behalf. If he winds up in the hospital again, God forbid, you have the authority to answer for him if he's unable to do so himself. You can always call me for advice, but you will be the one to sign any necessary papers and pay his bills while he is out of commission."

Gordon had listened to his sister, but he had not bothered to ask any of the questions that came to mind. He knew himself well enough not to. If he focused too hard on any one thing that Karen said, he would miss everything she said afterward. Furthermore, if he were to ask about something and later forget the answer he had been given, he would be chastised for not paying attention. For this reason, Gordon had adopted the practice of nodding now and asking questions later. That way, the decision could be made by Karen or someone else, and no blame would fall on him if something went wrong. This placed the responsibility on someone else—someone who was better equipped to make critical decisions. Gordon always did his best to avoid responsibility. He had a genuine aversion to it.

Gordon went straight to Cormack's and slapped a twenty on the bar. Mack glanced at the bill, and the look of annoyance on his face softened a little. The bartender twisted the cap off a bottle and exchanged the beer for the bill.

"Take what I owe from yesterday," Gordon said, lifting the bottle to his lips. "I'd have brought it to you last night, but I had to cash a check."

Mack rolled his eyes and rang up the beer at the register.

"A gift from your uncle?" Gordon's friend, Remmy, asked from his perch on a nearby barstool.

"Yeah, some gift." Gordon made a flapping sound with his lips. "I'm supposed to buy a rake. How much does a rake cost these days?"

"I don't know," Remmy confessed. "Hey, Mack. How much for a new rake?"

"Google it," Mack said as he placed five singles on the bar in front of Gordon.

"Five bucks?" Gordon said with genuine astonishment. "That's it?"

"Two shots and a beer," Mack said, crossing his arms over his chest. "Five bucks each at the happy hour rate. And that's without a tip."

"But I only had one shot," Gordon argued.

"Yeah, well, you bought one for Bill, too."

"I did?" Gordon asked, meeting Mack's judgmental scowl. "Oh yeah, I remember now," he said, despite having no real memory of it.

"Where are you gonna get a rake?" Remmy asked.

"Hardware store, I guess."

"It will probably be cheaper at Walmart," Remmy proposed.

"I hate Walmart."

Both men sipped their beers.

"How's your uncle doing?" Remmy asked. "Is he still in a wheelchair?"

"Yeah," Gordon said glumly. "They took the casts off his ankles, but he can't put any weight on them. They say he may never walk again."

"Damn. That sucks."

"Sucks for me too. I gotta do everything for him now."

"Everything?"

"Well, everything that requires two working legs. I gotta do all the shopping and put everything where he can reach it. Plus, I gotta do anything and everything that needs doing around the house."

"You can get a basic lawn rake for under twenty bucks at Walmart," Mack said without looking up from the smartphone in his hand. "Thirty at Salvatore's Hardware."

"Told ya Walmart is cheaper," Remmy said.

Gordon sipped his beer, silently calculating how much of Uncle Milton's money he could spend at the bar while still having enough left over to buy a rake. He removed the ten-dollar bill from his wallet and dropped it on top of the singles.

"Two shots of Jack, Mack," he said, confident that Remmy would return the favor.

3

Gordon climbed out of the sputtering Chevy and retrieved the rake from the back seat. It wasn't brand new, but it could easily pass for new from a distance. He had noticed the rake leaning against the side of a garage while driving to the store to replace Uncle Milton's cottage cheese and quickly turned around to seize the opportunity. He grabbed the rake, tossed it into the backseat through the open driver's side door, and proceeded to the store. He bought cigarettes and a twelve-pack of beer with the money he no longer needed for a rake and was so absorbed in his good fortune that he nearly walked out of the store without the cottage cheese. He drove to Uncle Milton's in high spirits, and two beer cans lay empty on the floor of the backseat by the time he pulled into the driveway. As he carried the rake to the backyard, Gordon accidentally bumped into the side mirror of Uncle Milton's Cadillac. The car was one of Uncle Milton's most prized possessions, so Gordon felt relieved to discover that the mirror was loose but still intact. The door of the rusty old shed squealed as he pulled it open, and Gordon jumped back with a squeal of his own when a black cat bolted out, darting between his legs.

"Ah! You little fucker!"

The cat jumped onto the four-foot fence separating Uncle Milton's yard from the neighbor's, where it stopped to casually lick a front paw. The feline balanced effortlessly on the horizontal beam while stretching its body, behaving as if it hadn't been terrified just five seconds earlier. Gordon made a hissing sound and waved the rake in the air, but the cat appeared unfazed. Gordon tossed the rake into the cluttered shed, slamming the door loudly enough to make the cat flinch.

"Tough guy, eh?" he muttered, narrowing his eyes at the animal. "You know I hate cats, right?"

Gordon began walking back down the driveway toward his car, then suddenly lurched toward the fence with his hands curled into claws. The cat leaped down into the neighbor's yard and then abruptly paused to look back after a few short strides. Gordon presented his middle finger to the indifferent feline before grabbing the cottage cheese from the car on his way to the front door.

"Where've you been all day?" Uncle Milton grumbled from his usual position in front of the TV.

"I had to go to the bank, shop around for a decent rake, then get your cottage cheese." Gordon held up the container, but his uncle's eyes remained glued to the news program on the TV.

"And that takes all day?"

Gordon offered no response. He had slept in, which was typical for a Saturday, then spent much of the afternoon at Cormack's. More than half of the money his uncle had given him was gone by the time Bill showed up to repay the shot that Gordon had no memory of buying him the day before. He managed to coax a beer out of Bill to chase down the shot, and the late November sun was teasing the horizon by the time he left the bar.

"Is there something else you wanted me to do?" Gordon asked as he opened the refrigerator and put the cottage cheese inside.

"I need you to check the boiler."

Gordon felt a sinking feeling in his gut. Checking the boiler would require him to go into the cellar. Gordon had hated and feared Uncle Milton's cellar since childhood, and that fear remained with him to this day. It was an unreasonable fear, particularly for a middle-aged man, but it persisted nonetheless.

"Check it for what?" he asked.

"Check the temperature and the pressure on the gauge. The proper settings are written on a piece of paper on the rafter above it. Make sure they're within the indicated range." Uncle Milton turned the wheelchair to face the kitchen doorway. "It's been getting colder at night, and I don't want the old girl crapping out on me."

Gordon turned toward the cellar door next to the refrigerator, doing his best to suppress the childhood dread that washed over him. "What happens if you don't check it?" he asked. "Will it blow up or something?"

"It'll shut down if the pressure gets too high. The oilman installed some kind of governor gadget on it a few years ago when I refused to buy the new furnace he was trying to sell me. They always want you to buy new, whether you need it or not. The old girl still heats the house, but now she automatically shuts down when the levels exceed the safe range. I had him back to fix it, but he says that goddam governor is the only way to keep the boiler up to code. The oil delivery guy checks it when he comes to refill the tank, and he'll fuss with the valves if anything is off, but he only comes when I call. I won't sign up for their regular deliveries. They fix the prices, you know. You don't know what you're paying until you get the bill. You have to watch the price of oil and buy low." Uncle Milton rolled into the kitchen and nodded toward the cellar door. "Check the oil level on the tank, too," he said. "Write it down if you have to."

"I'll remember," Gordon said, as he opened the door.

The old doorknob rattled loosely in Gordon's hand. All the doorknobs in Uncle Milton's house were loose and clanky from decades of use. Musty air wafted out of the darkness, and light from the kitchen's overhead fixture illuminated the inside wall. Various things had been written on the wall above the light switch, some in pen, some in pencil. Gordon assumed they'd been put there by previous owners since the most prominent of them was the word "COAL," followed by a series of tally marks. The old coal furnace had been replaced before Uncle Milton moved in, so it stood to reason that they were responsible for that one. There was some faded pencil scribbling that was illegible, along with a series of three numbers separated by dashes, written in black pen or marker. Gordon thought that the numbers 12-3-64 represented a date, possibly indicating when the old residents moved out or when Uncle Milton had moved in.

"Don't tell me you're still afraid of the cellar," Uncle Milton huffed. "You're a grown man, for chrissakes!"

"I'm not afraid," Gordon said, sounding overly defensive. "I was just reading that stuff on the wall."

"Never mind that. Get on down there. Do you need a pen and paper to write it down?"

"No, I can remember a number alright."

Gordon flipped the wall switch and descended the stairs, keeping one hand on the cool stone block wall. The only light source was a single bulb mounted to one of the exposed joists near the center of the cellar. Gordon's head just cleared the crossbeams, but they were low enough to compel him to walk with a slight hunch. The boiler and the oil tank stood side by side against the back wall, and Gordon leaned to one side to keep his shadow off the gauge. He had to squint to read it. His eyesight continued to worsen with each passing year, but he had yet to visit an eye doctor. Gordon was not one to keep up with routine health checkups. He compared the pressure and temperature readings with the numbers on the paper tacked to the wooden beam above the boiler. They didn't match exactly, but he considered them close enough to pass as acceptable. The gauge on the oil tank indicated that it was slightly more than a quarter full.

Turning around to leave, Gordon's eyes fell on the small door under the stairs. The door was half the size of a standard one and was secured with a latch and padlock. Gordon had been both curious and frightened of that little door as a child. He imagined that a half-sized troll or some other monstrosity was locked behind that door, waiting to be set free. Looking at it now, those memories returned, and though he no longer believed in such nonsense, Gordon hurried to the foot of the stairs. He recalled the time when his cousin, Jerry, had talked him into going into the cellar with him, and a loud banging sound had sent them both running for the stairs. Jerry flew up the stairs first and burst into the kitchen, but Gordon tripped on his way up, banging his chin hard on one of the steps. He scrambled the rest of the way up with his hands on the steps in front of him and tumbled onto the kitchen floor. Gordon's mother and Uncle Milton rushed in to see what all the commotion was about, and everyone noticed the blood at the same time. Gordon's mother attempted to stop the bleeding at the kitchen sink while Uncle Milton ranted and raved about his nephews going into the cellar. Jerry attempted to make excuses, trying to explain the banging they had heard, but that only seemed to further anger Uncle Milton. Gordon had to be taken to get stitches, and both boys were assigned a list of chores to be done the following weekend as punishment. Sometime later, Gordon had asked his uncle what was behind the little door, but his answer only added to the mystery. "Never mind what's behind that door," he'd said. "It's none of your business. Leave it alone and stay out of the cellar."

Gordon was slightly out of breath when he returned to the kitchen, and Uncle Milton noticed.

"You'd better give up those cancer sticks, Boy," he said. "When I was your age, I could run up and down those stairs without getting winded."

Gordon switched off the light and closed the cellar door without responding, knowing it would only invite more haranguing.

"Were the levels good?" Uncle Milton asked.

"Everything's fine," Gordon said, leaning his shoulder against the door until the latch clicked into place.

"How much oil's in the tank?"

"More than a quarter."

Uncle Milton grunted. "That means I still have some time before I have to place an order."

Gordon thought a quarter tank should last all winter long, considering how cold his uncle kept the house. He was a miser in all ways. "Do you need anything else before I go?" he asked, eager to get back to The Dump with his beer.

"Where's that new rake?"

"I put it in the shed."

"Well, the yard needs raking," Uncle Milton said, turning the wheelchair and rolling back into the living room. "You can do that tomorrow morning."

Gordon's shoulders sagged. He liked to sleep in on Sunday mornings. "I'll get here when I can," he said, pulling open the front door. "I got stuff of my own to do."

"What the hell do you have to do on a Sunday morning?" Uncle Milton grumbled, resuming his place in front of the TV. "Are you going to church? Have you found Jesus or something?"

Gordon ignored his uncle's attempt at humor and shut the door behind him.

4

Gordon splashed cold water on his face and slicked back his thinning hair. His reflection in the bathroom mirror looked old and tired, with two days' worth of stubble on his face and neck that would remain for the day, since he rarely shaved on weekends. Moving to the kitchen side of the one-room apartment, Gordon fetched some chocolate chip cookies from a cabinet, popped one in his mouth, then dropped the package on the table. He chewed the cookie while grabbing a container of milk from the otherwise empty refrigerator and drinking directly from the carton. He sat down at the table and continued eating until all the cookies were gone. He finished what was left of the milk and threw the empty carton at the garbage can, missing it by a long shot.

"Fuck you," he said, directing the expletive at both the carton and the receptacle.

With breakfast out of the way, Gordon pulled on the same pair of jeans he'd worn the day before and fished a clean T-shirt out of his dresser. He put on his jacket and stepped outside onto the wooden landing.

"Have you got the rent for me, Gordon?"

Gordon turned to the source of the voice and found his landlord, Mr. Crutch, standing in the driveway below.

"Uh, not yet, Mr. Crutch," Gordon said, descending the stairs. "Like I said the other day, I'll have it for you by the end of the week."

"It was due two weeks ago, Gordon. I'm not going to let you keep taking advantage of me." Mr. Crutch said, louder than necessary. "There are other people I could be renting to. Reliable ones who like to pay their rent on time."

"I said I'll have it," Gordon said, wishing he'd done a better job of hiding his annoyance.

"You have until Friday. If you don't have the rent by then, I *will* evict you."

Gordon walked past his landlord and got into his car without saying another word. He drove to Uncle Milton's house, fetched the rake from the shed, and went right to work moving leaves, hoping to have a fair amount of work done before Uncle Milton noticed he had arrived late. The fenced-in backyard was very small, so it wasn't long before Gordon had most of the leaves piled up in the driveway. He turned at the sound of a window opening and found Uncle Milton peering out at him.

"I guess you went to church after all, eh?" he taunted. "Either that, or you slept half the day away."

"I told you I had stuff to do," Gordon said. "It's getting

done now, so what's the difference?"

Uncle Milton grunted and slid the window down. Gordon raked and kicked the leaves to the curb until the driveway was mostly clear, then quickly attended to the tiny front yard. On his way back to the shed, the next-door neighbor, Shirley, stepped out onto her porch.

"Hello, Gordon," she said, pulling a button-down sweater around her ample shoulders. "How's your uncle doing?"

"Hi Shirley," Gordon said, pausing partway down the driveway. "He's his usual grumpy self."

Shirley smiled sympathetically. "Well, you'd be grumpy, too, if you were confined to a wheelchair for so long."

"Yeah, I guess."

"He never shoulda been up on that ladder at his age," Shirley said, shaking her head. "What on earth was he thinking?"

"I don't know," Gordon said with an exaggerated shrug. "I told him I would clean those gutters, but nothing can ever be done fast enough for him."

"Is he getting any better? Do the doctors think he'll be walking any time soon?"

Gordon shrugged again. "Don't know. Both his ankles are messed up pretty bad. We'll just have to wait and see, I guess."

"Well, you tell him I was asking about him," Shirley said, slowly making her way down the front steps one at a time.

Gordon said he would, then continued down the driveway to the shed. A pair of cats watched him from the other side of the fence, and Gordon would have given them a scare if Shirley weren't still within earshot. He put the rake in the shed and then entered Uncle Milton's house through the back door. He scanned the kitchen countertops for something to eat and picked up an unopened box of graham crackers. Uncle Milton rolled in from the living room just as he was tearing the box open.

"If you opened it correctly, you could seal it back up with the flap on top," he said, scowling. "Why do you have to make a mess of everything? You're like a one-man wrecking ball."

Gordon placed the box of crackers back on the counter without taking one. "I worked up an appetite, and I haven't had lunch yet. I sure could go for a burger," he said, hoping his uncle would take the hint and throw him a few bucks.

"Did you get the leaves out from behind the shed?" Uncle Milton asked, ignoring the hint.

"Yeah, I got 'em," Gordon lied. "It's all done."

"Those leaves will just blow out from back there if you don't rake 'em out," Uncle Milton pressed.

"I said I did it."

Uncle Milton grunted, straining to lift himself high enough in his wheelchair to see out the window above the kitchen sink. Gordon knew he was searching for something else to complain about and was likely trying to invent another chore to assign to him. Gordon just wanted to get the hell out of there, get a bite to eat, and pop into Cormack's for a beer. He just needed some money, which Uncle Milton should have already offered for all the hard work he'd just done, but the old miser always made him ask for it.

"Can you spare a couple of bucks so I can get some lunch?" he asked, pretending to brush something off his shoulder. "I don't have any cash on me."

"You never have any cash on you," Uncle Milton huffed, turning the wheelchair in place. "You're gonna suck me dry, Boy."

Gordon opened the crackers and shoved one into his mouth, hoping to finish chewing before Uncle Milton returned from his bedroom with the money. He closed the tattered lid and pushed the box toward the back of the counter just in time.

"Here," Uncle Milton said, holding out two twenties. "Don't spend it all at that shithole bar."

Gordon accepted the bills with a nod, not wanting to speak through the partially chewed cracker still in his mouth. Uncle Milton's voice followed him out the front door.

"I mean it!"

5

"Do you know anything about power of attorney?"

"Isn't that just giving someone authority to make decisions for someone else?" Remmy suggested from the barstool directly beside Gordon's. "So they can sign papers and stuff for them?"

"Yeah, but what does it mean as far as money and bank accounts?" Gordon pressed. "What about all that?"

"Yeah, that too, I guess," Remmy said thoughtfully. "They should be able to sign checks and pay bills while the person is out of commission. I think that's the whole point of it."

"What if the person isn't out of commission?" Gordon took a long swig of beer and clunked the empty bottle down on the bar loud enough for Mack to hear.

"Then I guess there's no reason for it," Remmy said with a dismissive shrug.

"It's when someone delegates authority to another person to make decisions on their behalf," Mack said, popping the lid off a fresh beer and placing it in front of Gordon. "It can be implemented for a variety of reasons."

"Like what?" Gordon asked, pulling the fresh beer close.

"People typically set up a POA when someone is sick or incapable, like Remmy said, but it can be arranged beforehand so that it's already in place if things take a turn for the worse." Mack leaned back against the counter, crossing his arms. "I have a POA set up with my mother."

"Why's that?" Remmy asked. "Is your mom sick or something?"

"She has early dementia," Mack said, shifting his gaze to an empty corner of the bar. "She's okay most of the time, but the doctors say it will only get worse. I already started helping her with paying bills. She forgets sometimes."

"Did they put your name on her checks?" Gordon asked.

Mack looked suspiciously at Gordon. "Yeah, we created a joint account. Why do you ask?"

"My uncle did the same thing with me. It was my sister's idea. She lives in Colorado and thought I should do the power of attorney thing for him." Gordon lifted his beer to his lips. "I already do everything else for him."

"Does your uncle have a lot of money?" Remmy asked. "Is he rich?"

"No, not rich," Gordon said thoughtfully. "But I really don't know how much he has. He's a real miser, so he might have a secret stash hidden away somewhere."

"Well, if your name is on the account, you should be able to see for yourself. You can find out how much he's got in the bank." Remmy flashed a mischievous grin. "And then you could clean him out and buy drinks for the whole bar!"

Mack narrowed his eyes at the two men. "Don't do anything stupid, Gordo," he said. "Not only is it wrong, but you can get in a lot of trouble for taking advantage of a situation like that. A power of attorney allows for honest mistakes, but not for deliberate theft."

"I would never do anything like that," Gordon said, lowering his eyes to his beer.

Remmy and Mack shifted the conversation to pensions and the pros and cons of union jobs, but Gordon remained preoccupied with his own thoughts.

6

Gordon grabbed a package of cookies and a container of chocolate milk from the lunch truck that parked in the lot behind the warehouse every morning. He presented the items to Rafi, the truck's owner, who added them to Gordon's weekly tab. He took his breakfast into the warehouse and sat down on a short stack of pallets next to Otis, the only employee older than Gordon.

"Breakfast of champions," Otis said, shaking his head as Gordon ripped open the wrapper and stuffed an entire cookie into his mouth. "Are you ever gonna start taking care of yourself? You eat like shit, smoke like a chimney, and drink like a fish. You won't last long living like that."

"Life sucks, and then you die," Gordon said through a mouthful of mashed cookie.

Otis shook his head again. "Suit yourself. But you better cool out with the drinking at work."

Gordon shot a questioning look at his coworker.

"Suski found an empty bottle somewhere in the warehouse yesterday," Otis said, lowering his voice.

"He was asking around about it this morning. Be ready for it."

A buzzer sounded in the warehouse, and Otis stood up. "Here he comes now," he muttered quietly before turning and walking toward a nearby forklift.

"Do you know anything about this, Nagel?"

Gordon turned to find Lee Suski, the warehouse manager, standing with an empty half-pint bottle in one hand. Gordon recognized the vodka bottle but couldn't remember where he had left it or when. He squinted at the bottle as if trying to read the label.

"Looks like vodka," he said, feigning ignorance. "What do you wanna know?"

Suski glared at Gordon. "You know what I'm asking, Nagel. Someone was drinking on the job, and they're gonna get fired when I find out who it is."

"Well, it wasn't me," Gordon said, popping a second cookie into his mouth.

"There are only ten of you in the warehouse, so it's just a matter of time," Suski declared. "I've already reported it to HR."

"How do you know it wasn't someone from the front office?" Gordon asked, still chewing.

"Because it was in the fucking warehouse!" Suski barked. "Hidden behind some boxes on a pallet rack."

Gordon offered an innocent shrug. "Just sayin'," he said. "One of the suits from up front could have stashed it there."

Suski exhaled in frustration. "Get to work, Nagel," he said, eyeing the chocolate milk container in Gordon's hand with a look of disgust. "You're on the clock now."

During lunch break, Gordon overheard some of the younger guys discussing the incident at the picnic table behind the warehouse, noticing their furtive glances as he walked by. He picked up two hot dogs and a can of soda from the lunch truck and brought them to his car. He ate the hot dogs and then reclined the driver's seat for a short nap. He thought about the bottle he kept under the seat, and as much as he wanted to, he didn't reach for it like he usually would before returning to work. He couldn't risk Suski—or anyone else—detecting alcohol on his breath when he returned to the warehouse.

By quitting time, Gordon had developed a headache, and his hands were beginning to shake. He rarely went this long without a drink, and although he recognized the symptoms as early signs of withdrawal, his concern was focused solely on the remedy rather than the underlying cause. He was the first to clock out and leave the building. He drove out of the industrial park and pulled into the Duncan Donuts parking lot on Route 13. He fished the bottle out from under the seat, unscrewed the cap, and gulped down all that remained of the vodka.

Gordon didn't notice the police officer until he was standing directly beside his car.

7

Gordon woke up five minutes before he was supposed to be at work. He called Suski and told him he had a stomach bug and wouldn't be able to come in. Suski almost sounded triumphant as he informed Gordon that he had no sick or personal days left and would not be paid for his absence.

"I know," Gordon lied, "but I'm just too sick to come in. If I feel better later, I might come in for a half day."

"Don't bother," Suski said, then abruptly hung up.

Gordon dozed off again, then spent another two hours in bed watching TV after waking up. The morning game shows helped distract him from what had happened the day before, but reality hit during commercial breaks. The drinking that the police officer had witnessed was Gordon's first drink of the day, so he passed the inevitable sobriety test without issue. He was issued summonses for having an open container of alcohol and for drinking in public before being sent on his way. Despite his efforts, Gordon could no longer ignore his mounting problems. The rent was overdue and had to be paid by the end of the week. His bank account was virtually nonexistent, and he had just lost a day's pay. Suski was looking for any excuse to fire Gordon and had almost found one when he discovered that empty bottle in the warehouse. And now he had two expensive violations that would have to be paid in the very near future.

After finding nothing to eat in the refrigerator, Gordon heated some water and poured it into a cup of ramen noodles. While slurping down the salty soup, he checked the contents of his wallet and found only eleven dollars inside. He needed to get some money fast, and his best option was to call his sister and ask her to send him some. He would tell her his car required repairs and that fixing it was critical to caring for Uncle Milton. He dreaded making the call, but decided it was best to get it over with. Karen answered after two rings.

"Gordy," she said, sounding distressed. "I was just about to call you. I'm at the hospital with Nick right now. They found cancer."

Karen's voice hitched on the C-word. Gordon was caught off guard by the news and said the first thing that came to mind. "What kind?" he asked.

"Pancreatic. It's not good."

Karen started to sob. Gordon tried to think of something to say, but he had never been good with words, especially at times like these. "Is that a bad one?" he finally asked. "Can they cut it out?"

"It's one of the worst, and we don't know if it can be removed. It depends on how advanced it is. We're waiting to hear from the doctor. He's reviewing the results right now."

"Is he gonna..." Gordon trailed off, searching for the right words. "Did they say how long he has or anything?"

"No, they didn't say how long, you insensitive prick!" Karen snapped, noticeably restraining herself from shouting. "They just found it! There will be some kind of treatment. We'll do whatever it takes to get through this."

Gordon winced, pulling the phone away from his ear. "Okay, okay," he said. "I don't know what I'm supposed to say."

"You never do."

"I'm sorry," Gordon said, though he didn't mean it. He never liked Nick and was sure the feeling was mutual. All he could think about was the money he so desperately needed and how to shoehorn it into the conversation.

"We'll get through this," Karen said, more to herself than to Gordon. "We'll find a way. We have to."

"That's good," Gordon said, absently eying the empty vodka bottle on the counter. "I'm still taking care of Uncle Milton here, which is why I called. My—"

"Don't tell me something happened to Uncle Milton," Karen interrupted. "I can't handle anything else right now."

"No, he's alright. I just—"

"Good. I'm going to need you to take care of him through the holidays. We obviously won't be able to fly in this year."

"Yeah, okay, but my car needs work, and I'm kinda short of funds right now."

Karen let out an exasperated sigh. "Oh, Gordy. When are you gonna pull your shit together? Why don't you use Uncle Milton's car? It's just sitting in his driveway, isn't it?"

"Yeah, but he won't go for that," Gordon said. "You know how he is."

"I'll talk to him. I have to tell him what's happened anyway. I'll try calling him later today."

Gordon liked the idea of commandeering Uncle Milton's car, but that wouldn't pay his bills.

"Okay, but I—"

"I have to go," Karen cut in. "The doctor is back."

Gordon left his apartment without bothering to take a shower and went directly to the bank. He entered his PIN and waited impatiently as the ATM dispensed two twenty-dollar bills and a receipt. He pocketed the cash and frowned at the balance printed on the receipt. There was nowhere near enough money for rent. His only shot at coming up with the full amount was to borrow it, and Uncle Milton was his last hope. If that failed, he would just have to give Mr. Crutch whatever he had and hope he didn't toss him out.

Gordon's stomach growled, prompting thoughts of

food—a problem he could actually resolve. He walked to the Burger King next to the bank and quickly devoured a Whopper, large fries, and a large Coke. Returning to his car, he slid the key into the ignition but did not immediately start the engine. He wasn't sure where to go. It was too early to go to Uncle Milton's house because he would want to know why Gordon wasn't at work. As usual, the question of when and where he would find his next drink arose, taking precedence over all others. He could buy some beer and bring it back to The Dump, but he might run into Mr. Crutch, whom he also wanted to avoid. He decided the best place to kill what was left of the afternoon would be Cormack's, and he turned the key.

Mack looked up from his cell phone as Gordon entered the near-empty bar. He popped open a bottle of Bud and slid it in front of Gordon's usual seat.

"Out of work early today?" he asked.

"Yeah," Gordon lied. "It was slow at the warehouse, so I cut out early."

Mack nodded and returned his attention to his phone. Gordon took a long swig and nodded to Collin, the only other patron at the bar. Collin responded with a slight nod of his own before returning his attention to the cable news program on the TV mounted in the corner. Collin was an old war vet who came in once or twice a week, nursed one glass of white wine, then left with a salute to Mack, who had also served in the military, half a century later in Iraq. Gordon attempted to engage the old man in conversation several times, but it never amounted to anything. He would either nod, shake his head, or shrug in response to anything said to him.

Now that he had some beer in his belly, Gordon's thoughts turned to his money situation and the last conversation he'd had in the bar regarding Power of Attorney. That led him to wonder if he could withdraw money from Uncle Milton's account. Gordon always used his ATM card whenever he needed cash from his own account and wondered if Uncle Milton had one—or if he could get one himself.

"Hey, Mack," he said. "Do you have an ATM card for that joint account you have with your mother?"

Mack's eyes flicked up from his phone. "Why do you want to know?"

"Just wondering. I'm always picking up stuff for my uncle, at least a few times a week, and I always have to go by his place first to get money from him. I just thought it'd be easier if I had an ATM card so I could get the cash myself. Save me a trip."

"I don't have one for my mother's account," Mack said, "but I guess you could get one. Anyone whose name is on a checking account should be able to. But you'd better ask your uncle first. It is his money after all."

"Oh, yeah. Of course," Gordon said, absently scratching the Budweiser label with his thumbnail.

8

Gordon pulled into the driveway behind Uncle Milton's car. He had never thought much of the old DeVille but saw it with new eyes now that he might soon be driving it. The Cadillac was at least twenty years old, but still in excellent condition; much better than Gordon's ratty old Caprice. He paused to admire the car before climbing the steps and letting himself in through the front door.

"I need you to check the boiler," Uncle Milton said the instant Gordon walked in. "I turned up the thermostat, but the radiators aren't warming up."

"Hello to you, too," Gordon said sarcastically.

"Are you sure the pressure was good last time? The radiators are cold as ice."

"Yeah, it was good," Gordon said, walking past Uncle Milton toward the kitchen. "I'll check it again, though. See if it changed any."

Gordon walked into the kitchen and opened the cellar door. He flipped the wall switch below the scribble on the wall and proceeded down the stairs before Uncle Milton had a chance to tease him about his childhood fear. Gordon heard the hissing of flames as he walked to the rear of the cellar and knew right away that the old boiler was working fine. The old carbon steel ticked and popped as he read the pressure gauge. The needle was in the desired range, just as it had been the last time. Gordon heard the telephone ring upstairs, followed by the sound of the cellar door closing. He turned to face the stairs, his nerves suddenly on edge. He knew Uncle Milton had to move the open door to access the old wall phone, but Gordon wished he hadn't closed it all the way. He chided himself for allowing his nerves to get the better of him, but his eyes still went directly to the little door beneath the stairs.

"Quit being such a wuss," Gordon said softly, hoping his voice would soothe his nerves.

Determined to confront his fear, he crouched down in front of the small door. He could hear Uncle Milton's muffled voice talking on the phone upstairs. He grabbed hold of the old padlock shackled to the metal hasp and tugged on it.

Something stirred on the other side.

Gordon fell back on his butt before quickly scrambling to his feet. He heard a shuffling sound and was sure he saw the door move slightly, as if something had bumped into it from the other side. He shot up the stairs, grabbing for the doorknob as soon as it was within reach. He pushed the door, but it opened only partway, blocked by Uncle Milton's wheelchair on the other side.

"What in blazes is wrong with you, Boy!" Uncle Milton bellowed.

Gordon looked back down into the cellar, expecting to see something creeping up the stairs, but saw nothing.

"Hold on, Karen," Uncle Milton said into the phone. "Your idiot brother's banging my wheelchair with the door."

Gordon pushed his way into the kitchen as soon as Uncle Milton was out of the way, turning off the light and closing the cellar door behind him.

"You really are a piece of work," Uncle Milton said, repositioning his wheelchair and lifting the phone from his lap. Gordon heard his sister's thin voice coming through the phone as Uncle Milton brought it to his ear. "Yes, everything is fine," he said into the receiver, his eyes still on Gordon. "You just take care of Nick, and I'll deal with the manchild over here."

Gordon walked into the living room and sat down on the couch. *What the fuck was that?* he wondered. *Is there really something living under the stairs?* Gordon heard the phone clunk back into place on the wall, and Uncle Milton wheeled into view in the kitchen doorway.

"I can't believe you," he said. "A grown man, pushing sixty, still afraid of the cellar. Are you ever gonna grow up?"

Gordon considered telling his uncle that he'd heard something behind the little door, but knew that would only draw more reproach. "The pressure is fine," he said. "The boiler is heating up."

As if on cue, the radiator began to tick and tap. Uncle Milton wheeled over and tentatively touched the painted metal before fully resting his hand on it. He gave a satisfied nod and then turned the wheelchair to face Gordon.

"Your sister says you want to borrow my car," he said. "I guess you didn't have the balls to ask me yourself?"

"It was her idea," Gordon said innocently. "I'd be fine just fixing mine, but I don't have the money right now."

"Of course you don't. What's wrong with it?"

Gordon didn't have a specific response ready, so he said, "A bunch of stuff."

"A bunch of stuff," Uncle Milton echoed, a look of disgust on his face. "And how much will it cost to fix 'a bunch of stuff?'"

Gordon shrugged. "I don't know, exactly. I'd have to take it to the garage and have them look at it. And you know how that goes. They'll find one thing and then another, and—"

"All right, listen." Uncle Milton interrupted, "Take that piece of shit of yours to the garage tomorrow and have them look it over. Tell them not to do any work until they give you an accurate estimate. If it's reasonable, I'll loan you the money to get it repaired. In the meantime, you can drive the Caddy. But no drinking when you're driving my car." He pointed an accusatory finger at Gordon. "I mean it. If I catch one whiff of booze on your breath, the deal is off."

"Okay," Gordon agreed, "no problem. I'll drop the car off at the garage after work tomorrow." He stood and started walking toward the door. "Do you need anything else before I go?"

"What do you mean, anything else? You haven't done anything yet." Uncle Milton's wheelchair turned in place, and he rolled back into the kitchen. "Get me a pot pie out of the freezer. Then get the towels out of the dryer and put 'em up in the bathroom."

Gordon removed the frozen dinner from the freezer, unpackaged it, and placed it in the microwave. He set the timer and then went into the small laundry room off the kitchen, where he set about folding towels on top of the dryer. Uncle Milton continued to recite a list of chores for Gordon to do, clearly making them up on the fly as he tried to get as much as possible in return for allowing his nephew to borrow his car. But Gordon didn't mind. He was getting more than he'd hoped for.

9

Gordon popped a handful of breath mints into his mouth before opening the passenger-side door. "Thanks for the lift, Remmy," he said, getting out of the car. "See ya tomorrow." He drew a deep breath as his drinking buddy drove away, feeling the peppermint-scented air on the back of his throat. He hoped the mints and his beverage choice at the bar would mask any scent of alcohol on his breath. Remmy had been just as surprised as Mack when Gordon ordered a vodka and tonic instead of his usual beer and a shot at Cormack's. He told them he was just in the mood for something different, but the truth was he had heard that vodka didn't linger on the breath as much as beer or other types of alcohol. He bought the mints at the 7-11 next door to the service station after dropping off his car, and Remmy drove him to Uncle Milton's after following him there from the bar. He needed to appear sober if he hoped to drive away in the Cadillac and knew he would be forced to walk home if Uncle Milton suspected he had been drinking. Gordon walked through the front door just in time to hear his uncle shout, "Kalamazoo!" at the TV.

"I just dropped the car off," Gordon said, closing the door behind him. "I thought I'd go start the Caddy to make sure she's running alright."

Uncle Milton turned the wheelchair to face Gordon. "You just ran it in the driveway last week," he said. "She'll start up fine, as always."

"Yeah, I suppose," Gordon agreed. Uncle Milton made him start the car in the driveway about once a week. He believed an engine needed to be turned over regularly to stay in working condition. "What do you need me to do before I go?"

"You just got here for chrissakes!" Uncle Milton barked, pointing the wheelchair toward the kitchen. "Why are you always in such a hurry?"

"I didn't know you liked my company so much," Gordon said in a rare attempt at levity.

"I don't," Uncle Milton said over his shoulder. "But there's stuff that needs doing before you cut out. Wednesday is garbage night, in case you forgot, so you can start by taking the trash out."

Gordon removed the plastic liner from the kitchen waste basket and carried it outside through the back door. He lifted the lid off the garbage can beside the shed and yelped when an orange tabby bolted out from behind it.

"Mother fucker!" Gordon spat, swinging the plastic bag at the fleeing feline. "Fucking things are everywhere."

Gordon hated cats, dogs, and all kinds of pets. In fact, he had an aversion to animals in general. He dropped the bag inside the garbage can and carried it down the driveway, slowing to admire the Cadillac as he passed it by. He was looking forward to driving a reliable vehicle. He left the can at the curb and reentered the house through the front door.

"I need one of those dinners out of the freezer," Uncle Milton said from the kitchen. "And put a new roll of toilet paper in the bathroom."

Gordon put a frozen entrée in the microwave and fetched a toilet paper roll from the hall closet. He placed a fresh bar of soap on the sink as well, going the extra mile for his uncle on this special day. He proceeded to do a few more simple chores, feeling his uncle's eyes on his back all the while.

"How many drinks have you had today?" Uncle Milton asked.

"None," Gordon lied. "You said no drinking before driving the Caddy, so I skipped the bar today."

"Then what took you so long to get here after work?"

"I had to drop my car off at the garage. I had to wait a while to talk to the mechanic," Gordon lied again, "and it took longer than I wanted."

Uncle Milton made a grumbling sound in his throat, and Gordon turned to find scrutinous eyes on him.

"All right," he said, "I'm going to let you drive my car, but you're only to drive it home, to work, and back here." Uncle Milton's face scrunched up as if speaking the words pained him. "And to the store and back if your car isn't ready by Friday."

"That's fine," Gordon said. "I never go anywhere anyway."

"You go to that shithole bar all the time! You reek like booze and cigarettes every time you walk into this house."

"I don't go all the time," Gordon said, waving a dismissive hand in the air. "I stop in for a beer after work every now and then. That's all." He saw that Uncle Milton was about to say something, so he quickly added, "Don't worry. I won't go there while I have your car."

"You'd better not," Uncle Milton grumbled. "The key is in the junk drawer," he said, nodding toward a drawer beneath the counter.

Gordon opened the drawer and began shifting tools, rolls of tape, and other miscellaneous items around as he searched for the keys.

"They're in the box in the back."

Gordon reached to the very back of the drawer, pulled out a small metal box, and thumbed the lid open. The box contained several loose keys, including one attached to a ring bearing the Cadillac emblem. Gordon removed the car key and asked, "What are all these other keys for?"

"None of your business," Uncle Milton said,

squinting at the key in Gordon's hand. "Don't lose it."

"I won't," Gordon said, moving toward the back door.

"Go out the front," Uncle Milton said. "I already locked that one."

Uncle Milton turned the wheelchair in place and rolled into the living room. Gordon followed him out of the kitchen and offered a quick thanks before leaving. He slowly backed the Cadillac out of the driveway, assuming his uncle was watching from one of the windows. He slowly pulled away, circled the next block, and drove directly to the liquor store.

10

Gordon grabbed a sandwich at the lunch truck and headed for the Caddy in the parking lot. The guys had all come over to look at Gordon's new ride in the morning, and though he had enjoyed the attention, he now wanted to be left alone. He listened to the radio as he ate his lunch in the car, wishing he could change the presets to suit his taste. *Soon enough,* he thought. *This car will be all mine when Uncle Milton croaks.*

The thought set Gordon's mind to thinking about Uncle Milton's house and the improvements he would make when he inherited the property. The first thing he would do is paint the walls in colors of his choosing. Then he would fix up the kitchen, remove the old linoleum, and lay down new tile. Envisioning the kitchen conjured the image of the cellar door and what lay beyond it. He tried to think of ways to make the cellar less spooky, but couldn't think of any. He thought about the little door with the padlocked latch. He thought about the keys he had seen in the little box in the kitchen drawer and wondered if one of them fit the padlock. If so, would he open that door once the place was his? Could he?

Gordon shivered at the thought, and his optimism reversed course. He thought about the old furnace and the maintenance it constantly required. Could he even afford to buy the oil? Could he afford any of the upkeep at all? There would be utility bills and others that he probably didn't even know about. He would have to pay taxes. He would be required to do a lot of things—too many things. He didn't want that kind of responsibility. He hated responsibility.

There's a bottle of vodka in the trunk.

The thought blew into Gordon's mind like a welcome breeze. It promised immediate relief from stress and worry. It would dispel those negative thoughts and replace them with simple, manageable ones. It would make things better.

Gordon placed the half-eaten sandwich on the dashboard and pulled the lever to release the trunk. He walked around to the back of the car and lifted the lid. Uncle Milton's trunk was mostly empty and well-organized. There was a neatly folded wool blanket, a roadside emergency kit, jumper cables, and plenty of empty space. Gordon reached into the well in one corner of the trunk and withdrew the pint of vodka he had stashed there. He unscrewed the cap and took a generous sip behind the open trunk lid. His concerns about the house immediately began to melt away. There was no need to worry about any of that now. Karen would handle all the details once they inherited the house. They would sell the old pile and split the money. She might even let him keep more than half since she didn't need it. Gordon's mind began to shift to what he would do with all that money when he heard a voice nearby.

"So this is the new ride, huh?"

Gordon froze. The open trunk lid obstructed his view, so he didn't see Suski approaching. He tried to recap the bottle but failed to do so before his supervisor appeared around the side of the car. The expression on Suski's face changed from cordial to severe the instant his eyes settled on the bottle in Gordon's hand. He reached out and wriggled his fingers until Gordon handed over the bottle.

"Go home, Gordon," he said flatly. "We'll discuss this tomorrow."

Gordon felt relieved to see that Mr. Crutch's car wasn't in the driveway when he got to The Dump. He grabbed the brand-new bottle of vodka and a two-liter bottle of Pepsi from the passenger seat and carried them upstairs to his apartment. He locked the door behind him and pulled the shade down on the room's only window to block out the sun. He removed the only two ice cubes from the tray in the freezer and dropped them into a plastic cup. He filled the cup halfway with vodka and topped it off with Pepsi. The drink was still fizzing when he brought it to his lips, causing his eyes to tear as he took several generous gulps. He found the TV remote on his unmade bed, sat down at the table, and began surfing through the channels. He settled on the least annoying program and gulped down the rest of his drink. The ice cubes were almost entirely melted, but they would have to suffice for the refill. He made the drink the same as before, put the soda in the fridge, and returned to his seat at the table. He repeated the process several times until the events of the day softened and blurred into oblivion.

11

Gordon felt his coworkers' eyes on him as he neared the lunch truck. He fetched his usual breakfast of cookies and chocolate milk and sat down on the pallet beside Otis. The younger workers talked in hushed voices at the picnic table, one or two occasionally glancing in Gordon's direction. He knew their behavior had everything to do with him getting caught with the bottle yesterday, and it only magnified his anxiety.

"I suppose I'm the talk of the town around here," Gordon said to Otis, tearing open the cookie wrapper.

"Yep," Otis confirmed between sips of coffee.

"Do you think Suski will fire me?"

"I suspect he'll want to, but he'll have to go through HR." Otis looked at the ground as he spoke. "Maybe Kate will pull for you."

"Nagel!"

Everyone turned to see Suski standing in the doorway of the warehouse. He waved for Gordon to follow him and then disappeared back inside. Gordon set his breakfast on the pallet and entered the warehouse.

"Come with me," Suski said, setting off toward the front offices.

Suski led them to the conference room door and ushered Gordon inside. Kate Fitzgerald, the human resources officer, sat at one end of the table with a folder open in front of her.

"Good morning, Gordon," she said. "Have a seat."

Gordon sat in the nearest chair, while Suski took a seat next to Kate.

"I guess you know why we're here," Kate said, sounding disappointed. "Drinking on the job is grounds for termination; however, there is one option available for you to retain your position. State law states that employees suffering from drug or alcohol addiction can resume work if they complete a program." Kate looked up from the papers in front of her and met Gordon's eyes. "Is that something you'd be willing to try?"

"If it means keeping my job, I would," Gordon said without much thought.

Kate shared a glance with Suski and nodded. "Good. I was hoping you would say that. You will be suspended from work for eight weeks, during which time you will be required to attend regular meetings. I have all the information here for you."

"I can't afford to be out of work for that long."

"You will receive disability unemployment during

that period, so long as you attend the meetings and show progress. It won't be your full pay, but it's something. I'll help you fill out the paperwork."

Gordon agreed to the arrangement, and Suski got up and left after telling Kate to call him if he was needed. Kate talked Gordon through the paperwork, but he paid little attention to what she said. His mind was already out the door and looking for something to temper his rising anxiety. He signed the forms where Kate indicated, and she gave him some papers to take with him, including vouchers that needed to be filled out and signed at the AA meetings to verify his attendance.

"Well, I guess that's everything," Kate said, closing the folder. "It's all up to you from here on out. I hope you get the help you need, Gordon. I really do."

Gordon wasn't sure if Kate was being sincere or not, but he nodded and left the conference room without another word. He avoided eye contact with anyone and everyone as he walked through the warehouse and out to his car. He drove out of the industrial complex and pulled into the same Dunkin' Donuts parking lot where he had taken the sobriety test just a few days earlier. He read the time on the dashboard clock before shutting off the engine. The liquor store would open in a little over an hour, but he wanted to wait as long as possible before buying his next bottle. Today, he would see how long he could hold out.

Gordon knew he had a drinking problem, but it

wasn't something he wanted to fix. Drinking was the one aspect of his life he actually enjoyed. He looked forward to that first beer at Cormack's every day. Of course, he would have a shot or two of something stronger as well, but that was just to take the edge off, a way to calm his shaky nerves. He was a naturally nervous guy. Guys like him needed something to even things out. Some people take pills. Gordon drank. What's the difference? Gordon had entertained this reasoning before. It was always present in the back of his mind, justifying his drinking. He knew he sometimes took it too far, but a lot of people did that. He wasn't so different.

Two hours later, Gordon woke with a stiff neck. He started the car and set off toward home, where he planned to kill the rest of the morning. He arrived at the dump to find a van parked on his side of the driveway. The van had the name "Master Key Locksmith" printed on its side. Gordon parked at the curb and got out. As he closed the car door behind him, Mr. Crutch and a man in coveralls appeared from around the side of the van.

"Unless you hand me the rent in full right now, you're out, Gordon," Mr. Crutch said, his cheeks reddening as he spoke.

Gordon didn't answer. He didn't know what to say. He just looked from his landlord to his apartment door above the garage.

"That's what I figured." Mr. Crutch said, gesturing to

the man standing beside him. "I'm changing out the locks. I'll give you twenty minutes to get your stuff out of the apartment. Anything you leave behind will be at the curb before the end of the day. You'll have the whole weekend to pick it up. The garbage men will take whatever is left Monday morning."

Gordon's eyes dropped to the ground. He knew there was nothing he could say to change Mr. Crutch's mind. A piece of yellow paper moved into his field of vision.

"I have to give you this," Mr. Crutch said, his tone more composed. "It's the eviction notice. I'm sorry, Gordon, but you left me no choice. I can't afford to let you stay."

Gordon didn't take the paper. Instead, he said, "Fuck you." He looked at the locksmith. "Fuck you, too."

The locksmith looked down at his feet, clearly uncomfortable with the situation. Gordon turned and started walking toward the Cadillac.

"I see you got a new car!" Mr. Crutch shouted after him. "Maybe you should have paid your rent instead!"

"Fuck you all!" Gordon shouted at the sky while pulling the car door open.

He got into the car and sped away, tires screeching on the pavement as he made a beeline for the liquor store.

12

After stopping at the ATM and the liquor store, Gordon headed to the supermarket to grab Uncle Milton's usual Friday fare. The weekly purchases rarely changed, so he referenced the wrinkled list of items he kept in his coat pocket as he walked the aisles. He was tempted to take a swig straight from the bottle after leaving the liquor store, but had somehow managed to resist. Despite how his day was going, Gordon was trying to delay that first drink for as long as possible. Each minute that passed felt like both a small victory and a countdown to the inevitable.

Gordon put the two bags of groceries in the back seat of the Cadillac and took out the sixteen-ounce bottle of Coke he had purchased for himself. He got behind the wheel and set the Coke next to the brown paper bag on the passenger seat. He began driving without a specific destination in mind. He just needed to find a place where he could have that well-deserved drink. After only a few blocks, he pulled into the local park near Uncle Milton's house and turned off the engine. Only one other car was in the parking lot, and its owner was letting a small white dog out of the back seat. Gordon watched idly as the man and his dog began walking the circuitous path around the park's perimeter. He took in the weathered picnic tables and park benches. The small brick building, once a public restroom, now served solely as a canvas for meaningless graffiti. The playground area had changed little since Gordon's childhood, and seeing it brought back many memories. He remembered how his mother used to take him and his sister to the park to play on the swings and climb on the monkey bars during their elementary school years. He envisioned his mother in his mind's eye, young and outwardly smiling, despite the pain always lurking behind her eyes. Gordon missed that version of his mother. It was the only version he wanted to remember.

The stroke had taken Gordon's real mother away. He no longer recognized the woman who occupied her body, and for that reason, he did not want to see her or even think about her. She had become a ghost, just like his father.

After the stroke, Gordon had to start his life all over. With the proverbial apron strings cut, he had no one else to lean on, and he had leaned heavily on his mother. She helped him with his bills, his rent, and anything else he asked for, despite having so little herself. Growing up, Gordon never received the good grades or accolades that seemed to come so easily to his sister, so his mother provided him with the extra support he so often required. She recognized his shortcomings and never pushed him too hard.

When he got into trouble, which was often, she was lenient with him. Things might have been different if he'd had a father figure in his life, for better or worse, but Gordon never gave it much thought. He had never known his father, and never would, which was fine with him. He stuck around after Karen was born but left while Gordon was still in the womb. His mother rarely spoke of him, despite Karen's persistent questioning, and Gordon was content to leave it at that. If his mother could live without him, so could he. But now she was gone too.

And Gordon could barely take care of himself.

Gordon eyed the bag on the seat beside him, the neck of the quart-sized bottle poking out of the top. He smacked down the inner voice that suggested he should wait a little longer and snatched up the bottle. He unscrewed the cap and took a long pull, his head craning back against the headrest. The virtually tasteless vodka felt smooth and cool as it slid down his throat. A gust of wind whipped up scraps of paper and plastic, carrying them across the field and leaving them clinging to the low chain-link fence. It looked like it might rain. Gordon looked over at the small covered area where he and his high school friend, Manny, would hang out and smoke cigarettes whenever it rained. Manny was Gordon's only true friend during his teenage years and believed they would stay friends for life. But then Manny enlisted in the Marines shortly after graduating from high school and went off to boot camp. Gordon had only seen him once since then, when he came home for a visit, but it felt as if he were a different person. He wouldn't even join Gordon for a drink to celebrate his return, claiming he had given up "all that stuff." Manny's family moved out of town around that time, and they never spoke again.

Gordon took another swig from the bottle while surveying the neighborhood surrounding the park. The rowhouses lining the streets looked old and weathered, their tenants clearly unconcerned about their outward appearance. One house displayed a sagging Christmas wreath on its door, and another a faded plastic Santa figure on the front stoop, but the decorations only added to the neighborhood's somber appearance. An overcast sky loomed over the dreary scene, reflecting Gordon's sullen mood. This was the poor side of town, and it showed. The houses on the north side were big and separated by expansive, manicured lawns. Unlike the one before him, the park in North Coddington was clean and well-maintained. The memory of one particular night in that park ignited like an unwelcome flame on a warm bed of coals.

Simpleton.

Another generous sip of vodka, and the memory was doused, whisked away like smoke in the wind.

Gordon lowered the bottle to his lap but kept his head against the headrest, his eyes closed. The liquor was working fast in Gordon's empty stomach. It entered his bloodstream by familiar means and made its way to his brain, where it systematically tripped synapses and neurotransmitters like a mad scientist in a horror film laboratory. Gordon's body relaxed, and his mind quieted. *"The more the better,"* said the inner voice that had successfully subdued and replaced the more responsible one. Gordon followed this advice without opening his eyes, his arm moving robotically to lift the bottle to his lips. This time, a rush of warmth rose from his stomach to his neck and cheeks, and Gordon lazily opened his eyes. He found the dog walker standing directly in front of his car, their eyes meeting briefly through the windshield. Gordon noticed the look of disgust on the man's face before he turned and continued walking toward his car. He dropped a bag of poop into a metal garbage can before picking up the little dog and placing it in the backseat. He shook his head disapprovingly as he drove away, and Gordon resisted the urge to flip him off. He knew the man had seen him drinking, and he didn't want to give him any more reason to call the cops on him.

After another swig, Gordon lit a cigarette and cracked the window to let the smoke out. The sharp edges of his thoughts dulled, and those long-ago memories retreated to the dark corner of his mind where they eternally lingered. He began evaluating his current issues from a new, albeit distorted, perspective. Worry transformed into anger; guilt shifted to blame. Everyone was overreacting, making mountains out of molehills. Mr. Crutch could have—

should have—given him more time to come up with the rent. It was the holiday season, after all. What kind of person throws someone out into the street two weeks before Christmas? And Suski didn't have to report him to HR. He could have given him a slap on the wrist and sent him home. And now they expected him to go through some AA bullshit.

"I'm not doing that," Gordon said to himself. "They can't make me."

Gordon had never attended an AA meeting, but he had plenty of preconceptions about what they were like. *All they do is sit around in a circle,* Gordon mused, *boohooing about their pathetic lives and why they drink. They pry into each other's lives, digging up things that don't deserve to see the light of day—things that ought to remain buried.*

Simpleton.

And they never stop wanting to drink. They fall off the wagon, cry about it at the next meeting, and start the process all over again. It doesn't work. It wouldn't work— even if I did want to quit.

Gordon took another slug of vodka, and a wave of nausea bubbled up from his gut. The liquor was proving too much for his empty stomach. He opened the bottle of Coke and took a few swallows, prompting a belch that instantly relieved his queasiness. Gordon's head was beginning to feel like a fishbowl, his thoughts swimming around like lazy goldfish. He decided to mix the vodka with the Coke, but he didn't want to spill anything in Uncle Milton's precious Cadillac, so he opened the driver's side door and awkwardly climbed out of the car, holding a bottle in each hand and the cigarette pinched between his teeth. He felt dizzy as he stood up and had to steady himself by leaning against the car. He poured some of the Coke onto the ground to make room and began replacing it with vodka. Clear liquid ran over his knuckles as it glugged out in uneven spurts, but enough found its way into the plastic soda bottle to refill it. Gordon rocked on his heels as he looked for a place to set down the bottles so that he could recap them, and only then did he see the police cruiser parked by the park entrance. The car rolled into the lot as if it had been waiting for Gordon to notice it.

"Fuck!"

Gordon's eyes flicked from the soda bottle in his left hand to the vodka in his right, realizing he was about to lose both. He turned away from the approaching vehicle and gulped down as much vodka as he could before his throat tightened, refusing to swallow any more. He heard the police cruiser pull up and stop directly behind the Cadillac as he staggered around the open car door, dropping both bottles into the garbage can. Soda fizzed out of the Coke bottle, gushing through the wire mesh and onto the pavement. A car door slammed.

"Gordon Nagel."

Gordon turned to squint at the police officer

approaching him.

"You don't remember me?" the officer asked, stopping a short distance away. "I'm Trey, Shirley Booker's son."

Gordon tried to focus on the police officer, but there were two of him, both too blurry to identify. He swayed and grabbed hold of the still-open car door to steady himself.

"My mother lives next to your Uncle Milton?" Officer Booker continued, phrasing it like a question.

"Oh yeah, thas right," Gordon slurred. "Trey Booger, Shirley's son."

"That's your uncle's car, isn't it?"

Gordon nodded. "Yep. Mine's in the shop."

"Listen, Gordon. I saw you drinking here, which I'm sure you know is illegal. I can look the other way about that since you're not holding anything." The officer's eyes turned to the garbage can and back. "But I can't let you drive away."

Gordon staggered back as Officer Booker reached in through the open door and removed the keys from the ignition. He closed the door and activated the lock on the keyring before handing the keys to Gordon.

"Leave the car and walk to your uncle's house. I'll put a notice on it so it doesn't get towed. You can come back for it tomorrow."

Gordon swayed in place, staring at the keys in his

hand as if seeing them for the first time.

"You can walk, can't you?" Officer Booker asked. "It's only a few blocks. The walk might do you some good."

"I need the groshees," Gordon said, pointing in the general direction of the back seat.

Trey peered through the car's side window and then took the keys from Gordon's hand. He unlocked the car and grabbed both bags of groceries from the back seat. They were double bagged, paper inside plastic, so he held the looped handles open for Gordon to grab hold of. Gordon ungainly accepted the burden, taking one bag in each hand. Trey locked the car once again and tucked the keys into Gordon's coat pocket.

"Now get going before I change my mind," he said. "Sleep it off at your uncle's house."

Gordon rocked in place for a moment, unsure if he should feel angry or grateful. He ultimately decided on neither and began following the last instruction he'd received. He zigzagged side to side as he left the park and crossed the street, glancing back once to see Officer Booker watching him before he turned the corner. The grocery bags in each hand acted as counterweights, helping him maintain his balance as the sidewalk tilted beneath his feet.

13

Gordon set the grocery bags down on the porch and began searching himself for the keys he usually kept in his pants pocket. He discovered them in a coat pocket and, after several attempts, successfully inserted the correct key into the lock. He turned the knob, pushed the door open, and then bent down to pick up the groceries. He lost all sense of balance as alcohol-thinned blood rushed to his head, causing him to tumble forward and fall into the house. He held onto the bags as he hit the floor, and several items spilled out.

"For chrissakes, Boy," Uncle Milton hollered from his usual place in front of the TV. "What the hell's the matter with you?"

Gordon awkwardly shifted onto his knees, using his elbow to close the door. He began collecting the spilled contents and stuffing them into the bags. A shadow fell over him, and Uncle Milton's slippered feet rolled into view. Gordon looked up to find two Uncle Miltons glaring down at him from his wheeled throne.

"Drunk again, I see," he said, shaking his two heads. "And you were driving like that? In my car? I ought to have you arrested."

Gordon didn't answer. He attempted to stand up but lost his balance and fell backward, hitting his head against the door. He grabbed hold of the doorknob and pulled himself up off the floor. He picked up the grocery bags and headed for the kitchen, swerving unsteadily around Uncle Milton. The living room and the doorway to the kitchen began to tilt to one side, and Gordon leaned the other way to compensate. He bumped his shoulder on the doorframe and almost dropped the groceries again.

"You're a fucking mess!" Uncle Milton barked, following Gordon into the kitchen. "You can't even walk!"

Gordon dropped the bags onto the kitchen table with a clatter and began removing the contents.

"Just leave it!" Uncle Milton barked. "You're liable to break something."

"Gotta put everthin' in er right place," Gordon slurred. "It hasa be perfect. Only one right way to do it." He picked up a box of cereal and tossed it onto the counter. He grabbed a package of graham crackers and threw it against the wall above the countertop. "There ya go. Right where it belongs."

"That's enough!" Uncle Milton growled. "I've had enough of you. Get the hell outta my house!"

"Cottage cheese in the fridge," Gordon said matter-of-factly. The container bounced off the refrigerator's closed door and fell to the floor with a soft thud.

"I'm calling the cops," Uncle Milton said, rolling toward the wall-mounted telephone. "You can spend the night in jail."

"Don't forget the pickles!" Gordon said with exaggerated bravado, holding the jar up like a prized possession.

Uncle Milton pulled the receiver down off the wall and pointed it at Gordon. "I don't know why I put up with you for this long, Boy. You're a worthless drunk. A complete waste of life." He turned his attention to the phone in his hand and began thumbing the push buttons.

And then the pickle jar was soaring through the air. Uncle Milton's neck made a soft cracking sound as it bent sideways under the force of the jar striking him in the temple. The jar appeared to hover in the air for an instant before falling to the floor and shattering. Uncle Milton's head drooped forward, and the phone fell into his lap, the hand that had been holding it twitching sporadically.

"How you like them pickles?" Gordon quipped, still not fully grasping what he had done.

He tried to fix his gaze on Uncle Milton, but the whole room morphed into a chaotic blur that tugged persistently in one direction. Gravity seemed to have gone mad, pulling Gordon sideways. He reached out blindly for something to grab onto, and his fingers closed around a cabinet knob somewhere above him.

Then everything went dark.

14

Gordon woke up on the kitchen floor. The air reeked of vinegar. He pushed himself off the linoleum and sat with his back against a cabinet. The overhead light seemed brighter than usual and stung his eyes. From where he sat on the floor, he could see Uncle Milton's wheelchair through the legs of the table in the center of the room. He could not remember how he'd come to be on the floor. He wanted to get up and find something soft to lie down on, but was reluctant to stand. His head felt as if it were filled with sloshing liquid, and everything in sight kept shifting to one side. He stared at Uncle Milton's wheelchair for a full minute before concluding that it was not moving. *What's he doing over there? Is he waiting for me to get up?* Gordon considered asking his uncle what had happened, but that would mean admitting that he'd blacked out. He shifted onto his knees and gripped the edge of the counter to help him stand up. The room swayed as the blood drained from his head, and he stood with both hands on the countertop until he was overcome with the urge to vomit. He staggered to the sink and dry heaved several times before producing a foul stream of bile. He turned on the faucet and palmed cold water into his mouth until the acidic burning in his throat subsided. Looking out through the window over the sink, he saw that it was fully dark outside, the backyard partially illuminated by the floodlight mounted above the back door. *Was it dark when I got here?* Gordon didn't think so. Questions tried to form in Gordon's clouded mind, but they were incomplete and made no sense. Remembering Uncle Milton's proximity, he turned to see if his eyes could provide answers that his brain could not.

Uncle Milton sat slumped in his wheelchair, his chin on his chest. Blood from a wound on his temple trailed down his neck and stained the collar of his fleece sweater. Pickles and shards of broken glass were scattered across the kitchen floor, and the vinegary smell he had noticed upon waking suddenly made sense. Taking in the rest of the room, Gordon saw groceries strewn randomly on the countertops and a cottage cheese container on the floor in front of the refrigerator. A cabinet door lay on the floor in the corner near where he had awakened, and he looked up to see exposed shelves where it had once been attached. He observed all of this with a numb detachment, his brain unable to reconcile the information his eyes were relaying to it.

Turning his back to the room, Gordon placed his hands on the countertop to steady himself. He shut his eyes, but that only intensified the sensation of being on a rocking ship. He took a glass from the doorless cabinet and brought it to the sink. He filled the glass with cold water and chugged half of it. He took several deep breaths to suppress the urge to vomit, and it eventually passed. He thought drinking something carbonated would help his stomach, but he did not want to go to the refrigerator. He didn't want to turn around.

Gordon pressed his memory, demanding that it give him something—anything. He remembered going to work in the morning, and a sickening sensation rose from his stomach when he recalled the meeting that ended with him being suspended. He remembered driving to The Dump, where Mr. Crutch promptly evicted him. He had bought groceries. He bought vodka. He was drinking in the park when a cop showed up: Shirley's son, Trey Booker.

Things got hazy after that. He was drunk—very drunk—but who could blame him after a day like that? Trey had let him go; told him to walk to Uncle Milton's. He couldn't remember walking to the house or coming inside. He had no memory of what had happened in the kitchen.

Gordon made himself turn around.

He looked at Uncle Milton slumped in the wheelchair, and then at the mess of broken glass and pickles on the floor. Gordon remembered pickles being one of the items he'd bought at the grocery store, but did not recall dropping them. *Had I thrown them?* He wondered. *Did I throw the pickle jar at Uncle Milton?*

Yes, you did.

The memory was vague, but brief snippets of throwing the groceries all over the kitchen flashed in his mind. He looked around and saw the evidence everywhere. He looked again at Uncle Milton and noted the bruise and blood on the side of his head.

I hit him with the pickle jar.

Gordon hurried over to the wheelchair, stumbling and catching himself on the back of a chair. The telephone lay in Uncle Milton's lap, the coiled cord stretching from the wall like an umbilical. He grabbed his uncle by the shoulder and tried to shake him awake, but that only caused him to tip sideways in the chair. "Wake up!" Gordon shouted, slapping Uncle Milton's cheek several times. Gordon staggered backward into the refrigerator and steadied himself by grabbing hold of the freezer handle.

"What did I do?"

You fucking killed him, that's what.

Gordon's mind reeled as cold realization hit home. He picked up the phone in his uncle's lap, knowing that he should call for help. He stared at the phone in his hand for a long moment before hanging it up in the cradle. Gordon was still very drunk and not thinking clearly, but he knew what calling the police would do. He would be charged with murder. He would spend the rest of his life in prison.

Gordon's mindset immediately shifted to self-preservation mode. This had to be covered up—made to look like an accident. *I'll make it look like he fell,* he thought. *Make it look like he hit his head while moving from the wheelchair to the tub or toilet.*

Gordon hurried to the bathroom, doing his best to avoid slipping in pickle juice or stepping on broken glass. Standing in the bathroom doorway, he tried to envision how he could place the wheelchair and Uncle Milton's body to create the scene, but concluded that the floor space was too small to accommodate both.

How else can I make it look like he'd fallen?

Gordon considered the stairs, but Uncle Milton could not use them and had not been upstairs since the accident.

What about the cellar stairs?

Gordon went to the cellar door and pulled it open. Darkness yawned below. Gordon's panicked mind decided that acting quickly would somehow make the fake tragedy seem more believable, so he chose to act without overthinking it. He got behind Uncle Milton's wheelchair and pushed it to the open doorway. He tipped the chair forward with enough force to send Uncle Milton's limp body tumbling headfirst down the stairs. Gordon tried to push the wheelchair in after him, but it was too wide for the opening. A wave of nausea rose violently from Gordon's gut, and he hurried over to the sink, where he expelled a stream of bile-tainted water. He turned around and was overwhelmed with the need to close the cellar door and forever hide his dark secret. He shoved the wheelchair aside, slammed the door shut, and slid one of the kitchen chairs in front of it. He stumbled into the living room, collapsed face-first onto the sofa, and fell into a drunken slumber.

15

Gordon stirred in the middle of the night, still half-asleep, and adjusted his position on the couch. His arm had been pinned awkwardly beneath his torso, and he briefly felt the sensation of pins and needles before falling back asleep. When he next woke up, his head was pounding, but he managed to slip back into unconsciousness once more. The third time he opened his eyes, all his senses came alive, forcing him to remain in the waking world. It took him a moment to realize he was in Uncle Milton's living room, but he could not remember why he was there. His current state made it clear he had been very drunk the night before, and while that was not unusual, it had never happened at his uncle's house. The pain in his head increased tenfold as he pushed himself into a sitting position. He was still fully dressed and wearing his jacket and work boots. Looking around, he noticed that the kitchen light was on. A sour, vinegary smell hung in the air, teasing at a memory just out of reach. He tried to recall what had happened the night before, but was unable to think clearly with the incessant throbbing inside his skull. He figured a tall glass of water and some aspirin would help him feel better, so he got up from the couch. His joints protested as he stood, and a wave of nausea joined the chorus of other bodily complaints. He walked slowly toward the kitchen, and Uncle Milton's empty wheelchair came into view beyond the doorway.

Gordon halted in his tracks, a sinking feeling in his gut telling him that something was very wrong.

Where is Uncle Milton? Why isn't he in his chair?

Gordon resumed walking again, his anxiety increasing with every step. As more of the kitchen came into view, he saw what looked like green turds scattered on the floor. There were also pieces of broken glass and some kind of liquid. It took a moment for his sight and smell to connect the dots and conclude that he was looking at the remnants of a broken pickle jar.

"What the hell happened here?" he muttered, even though he knew, on some level, that he was somehow responsible for it.

Stepping into the kitchen, Gordon took in the mess all around him. Food items were scattered randomly on the countertops and the floor. Two grocery bags rested on the kitchen table, one empty and the other yet to be unpacked. One of the cabinet doors had been torn from its hinges and lay on the floor in the corner. Gordon looked once more at Uncle Milton's empty wheelchair and felt a wave of anxiety wash over him.

Where the hell is he?

Gordon hurried to his uncle's bedroom, glancing into the empty bathroom as he passed the open door. Uncle Milton was not in the bedroom, and the bed was neatly made. Anxiety escalated to panic, and Gordon's skin began to tingle. His neck grew warm, and a high-pitched ringing started to swell in his ears. Despite his inability to remember, he knew he had done something terrible the night before. He suddenly felt lightheaded, and his bladder threatened to let go right where he stood. He turned into the bathroom and relieved himself in the toilet. He ran cold water into the sink and splashed some on his face. He found some Tylenol in the medicine cabinet and washed four tablets down with several palmfuls of water. Stepping out into the short hallway outside the bathroom, Gordon once again took in the scene in the kitchen. He noticed one of the kitchen chairs positioned in front of the cellar door, and a troubling memory began to take shape at the back of his mind.

"I put that there," he murmured to himself. "After closing the door. After I..."

After what?

Gordon moved to the door and pulled the chair out of the way. A sense of dread washed over him as he reached for the doorknob. He was beginning to remember. He opened the door. The light in the kitchen illuminated only the first few steps, so Gordon quickly flipped the wall switch before he lost his nerve.

Uncle Milton lay on his side at the foot of the stairs, his body curled into a fetal position. His eyes were closed, and if Gordon didn't know any better, he might almost believe he was peacefully asleep.

He's not sleeping. He's dead.

The ringing in Gordon's ears intensified, and his entire body went numb.

I killed him. I killed Uncle Milton.

Gordon closed the door and leaned against it. He closed his eyes while he waited for a wave of lightheadedness to pass. Images began flashing behind his eyelids—snippets of memories playing in no particular order. He saw Uncle Milton slumped in his wheelchair with blood on the side of his head and neck. He saw groceries flying around the kitchen and a pickle jar shattering on the floor. He saw Uncle Milton tumbling down the cellar stairs and vanishing into the darkness.

Gordon opened his eyes, and the state of the kitchen reinforced the chaotic memories he had just relived. The cabinet door in the corner triggered a memory of waking up on the floor at some point during the night, and he could only assume that he had torn it from its hinges when he had fallen. Much of the night was an inebriated blur, so he tried to recall what had taken place beforehand. He remembered buying the groceries and going to the liquor store. He remembered driving Uncle Milton's car to the park.

The car! Where's the car?

Gordon's hand flew to his pants pocket, but the keys were not there. He continued checking all his pockets as he hurried into the living room to look out the window that faced the driveway. The car was not there. "Where's the fucking car?"

It's still at the park.

Gordon suddenly remembered his encounter with a cop: Shirley Booker's son, Trey. He had caught Gordon drinking in the park and made him leave the car there. He couldn't recall walking to Uncle Milton's house, even though he had clearly done so. The pieces were starting to come together—at least some of them.

But where are the keys?

Gordon spun around and scanned the living room. He spotted the keys on the floor near the front door and quickly picked them up, concluding that he must have dropped them after letting himself in.

What else am I forgetting?

Sitting down on the couch, Gordon replayed the events of the day before, filling in the blanks until he had a reasonable approximation of all that had occurred. The day had started off badly enough, having been let go from work and getting evicted from his apartment, and things only got worse from there. He remembered very little after leaving the park, but the image of Uncle Milton slumped in his wheelchair with a bloody wound on his head became clearer as he pressed his faulty memory. Although he couldn't fully remember or explain the reasoning behind his actions, he recalled pushing Uncle Milton down the cellar stairs to make his death seem like an accident. Reflecting on it with a slightly clearer perspective, it made no sense at all. No one would believe that his uncle had accidentally slipped out of his wheelchair and fallen down the stairs. It was utterly ridiculous. Gordon lowered his head and buried his face in his hands.

So now what do I do? Do I call the police? Karen? What the fuck do I do?

Gordon patted the breast pocket of his denim jacket, feeling the need for a cigarette. He removed the crumpled pack and found one broken cigarette inside. He stood and started walking toward the front door before deciding to just light up inside the house. After snapping off the broken end, Gordon lit the remaining half of the cigarette. He knew he would need more smokes, regardless of what he would do next, and decided the first thing he should do was fetch the Caddy from the park and run to the store. Without another thought, Gordon headed out the front door, locking it behind him. He walked four blocks to the park and felt an incredible sense of relief upon seeing the car where he had left it. He drove to the convenience store, where he spent the last of his money on a package of cookies, a pint of chocolate milk, and a pack of cigarettes. He drove back to Uncle Milton's house and parked in the driveway. Shirley stepped out onto her front porch just as Gordon was getting out of the car.

"Good morning, Gordon," she said. "You're here early today."

"Uh, yeah," Gordon said, closing the car door. "I got a lot of stuff to do today."

"How's Milton doing?"

"He's uh, not feeling great today," Gordon said, inventing a story on the spot. "I think he came down with something."

Shirley looked appraisingly at Gordon. "You don't look so good yourself. Are you sick too?"

"No, well, maybe," he said. "I suppose I'm not feeling so great either. Whatever he's got is probably contagious."

"Well, you two feel better. Tell Milton I was asking about him."

Gordon said he would and went into the house, his heart pounding in his chest. He went to the window that faced the driveway and watched Shirley reenter the house with the newspaper she'd retrieved from the front steps. He assumed her son hadn't yet told her about the incident at the park and hoped he wouldn't. Not wanting to return to the kitchen, Gordon decided to eat his breakfast in the living room. He found the remote on the side table where Uncle Milton always kept it and switched on the TV. He half-listened to the morning news while he ate, and his stomach began to feel better. The news anchors and reporters spoke and laughed as if everything were normal, despite a murder having just occurred in Gordon's little corner of the world.

Because they don't know, Gordon reminded himself. *No one knows.*

He considered the conversation he'd just had with the next-door neighbor. He spoke to Shirley as though nothing had changed, and she believed him because she had no reason to doubt him; no reason to believe he had killed his uncle in a drunken rage and dumped his body in the cellar.

"No one has to know," Gordon said, testing how the words sounded aloud. "No one will know if I don't say anything."

Gordon walked into the kitchen, still chewing the last of the chocolate chip cookie. He surveyed the mess and thought he could have it cleaned up in short order. He moved Uncle Milton's wheelchair into the bedroom and began picking up the broken glass and pickles. He mopped up the brine and then went over the floor with a potent mixture of Pine-Sol and hot water. He returned to the living room while the floor dried, smoked a cigarette, and watched TV until the game shows started playing. He returned to the kitchen and arranged the items on the counters until everything appeared as it always had, except for the missing cabinet door. He thought about trying to fix it, but the hinges were bent, and Gordon had never been particularly skilled with tools, so he placed the door between the washer and dryer in the vestibule.

"Like nothing happened at all," he said to the empty room.

As he spoke the words, Gordon turned to the cellar door. He wished he could secure it, but there was no lock on the door. The image of Uncle Milton's body at the foot of the stairs appeared in his mind, and Gordon hurried out of the kitchen, eager to be away from the door and its terrible secret.

16

Gordon slid the brand-new debit card into the ATM and punched in the four-digit PIN. He entered the desired amount and collected the five crisp twenty-dollar bills. He took the printed receipt and confirmed that the balance matched what was written in Uncle Milton's checkbook ledger minus one hundred. He pocketed the money and headed for McDonald's with a spring in his step.

Obtaining the debit card proved more challenging than Gordon had anticipated. The teller informed him that he needed the account number, proof of address, identification, and Social Security number. The request reminded Gordon that his Social Security card and almost everything else that belonged to him were still at the apartment or had been left at the curb by Mr. Crutch. He told the teller he would return and set off for The Dump. He was relieved to find his belongings stacked beside the garage rather than on the side of the road. His clothes and bedding had been stuffed into three garbage bags, while the rest of his belongings, which didn't amount to much, were packed in boxes. The apartment had come furnished, so there were no large items to take. Gordon backed into the driveway and was in the process of loading up his stuff when Mr. Crutch came out of the house.

"I'm sorry about all this, Gordon," he said. "But I had no choice. I got bills to pay, too." He held out a small box for Gordon to take. "This stuff looked important, so I didn't want to leave it outside."

Gordon accepted the box and pulled up one corner of the folded lid. He found the small wooden chest where he kept his personal items tucked inside. He nodded but didn't say anything to his former landlord. Mr. Crutch stood there for an awkward moment before going back inside his house. Everything Gordon owned fit in the trunk and the backseat with room to spare. After loading the car, he drove to Uncle Milton's house and carried his belongings inside. He found the checkbook for the joint account in a desk drawer and returned to the bank with everything he needed to obtain his new debit card.

Gordon was famished by the time he sat down to eat and immediately dug into his meal. He'd ordered Chicken McNuggets along with his usual Big Mack and large fries, and he savored every bite. His mind was still all over the place with all that had happened in such a short time, but Gordon was beginning to see the bright side of things. Just yesterday morning, he was unemployed, homeless, and broke. Twenty-four hours later, he had a place to stay and access to a bank account with a fair chunk of change in it. The drunken episode that led to Uncle Milton's death still weighed heavily on him, but it was gradually receding to the back of his mind. Gordon was very good at keeping negative thoughts at bay, even the very bad ones.

Simpleton.

And if they became too much to bear, he could always drown them in alcohol. He still had no idea what to do in the long term, but his short-term needs were being met. He had plenty of time to sort it all out and decide what to do down the line. He had accomplished a lot in one day. It was time to celebrate.

It was midafternoon by the time Gordon bellied up to the bar at Cormack's, and his first beer quickly disappeared. The proverbial "hair of the dog" erased any lingering effects of the prior day's overindulgence, and he felt the tension ease in his shoulders. Remmy came in and sat down beside Gordon just as Mack was delivering his second beer.

"Hey, Gordy," he said. "How's things?"

"Pretty good, Remmy. How about you?"

Remmy shot Gordon a suspicious glance. "What's gotten into you? You win the lottery or somethin'?"

"Why do you say that?"

"Because you usually say, 'Same shit, different day,' or 'Go fuck yourself.'"

Gordon laughed. "Yeah, I guess," he said. "I suppose I'm just having a good day."

Remmy shrugged, and Gordon placed a second

twenty on the bar.

"This round's on me, Mack," he said. "And a shot for each of us!"

Mack looked at the money before placing two shot glasses on the bar. He filled them to the brim with JD and took one of the twenties.

"Here's to better days," Gordon said as both men raised their glasses.

"You sure you didn't win the lottery?" Remmy said after chasing his shot with the beer Mack placed before him. "One of those scratchers or somethin'?"

Gordon smiled, relishing the warming effect of the whiskey. He really was feeling good. He had a full belly and enough money to buy drinks for himself and his bar chum. He had a reliable vehicle and a warm bed to drive home to.

"How's your uncle doing?" Mack asked as he collected the empty shot glasses.

Gordon felt himself wince and hoped no one noticed. "Same as always, I guess."

Mack nodded at the money on the bar in front of Gordon. "I take it you got that ATM card you were talking about."

Gordon followed Mack's gaze. "Uh, yeah. As a matter of fact, I did."

"That explains a lot," Remmy said.

"Don't get the wrong idea, guys," Gordon said,

sounding more defensive than he wanted to. "This here's my money."

"I don't care whose money it is," Remmy said with a chuckle. "As long as it keeps turning into beer and shots."

"Next round's on you, bitch," Gordon said while avoiding Mack's suspicious gaze. "I'm actually moving into my uncle's place to make caring for him easier. It's a lot of work, but I'll be living rent-free, so I'll have a little more money in my pocket from now on."

Gordon smiled as he thought about what he'd just said. His cover story was practically writing itself. And it kept sounding better and better.

17

Gordon saw Shirley walking up the steps of her front porch as he pulled into the driveway, prompting him to leave the beer he'd bought in the backseat for the time being. They exchanged greetings as Gordon got out of the car, and he thought it was as good a time as any to tell her he had moved into Uncle Milton's house.

"Looks like we're gonna be neighbors," he said. "I'm gonna be staying here full-time from now on."

Shirley paused on the top step, her breathing labored from the climb. "Why's that, Gordon? Is Milton not doing well?"

"Well, he's not getting any better. That cold or flu thing he got is still lingering. We just decided it would be easier if I moved in. The lease was up at my place anyway. My stuff's already inside."

"Oh, I see. Has he seen a doctor yet?" Shirley asked. "Us older folks don't handle germs so well. It could turn into something serious."

"I will if he gets any worse," Gordon assured, "don't you worry. I'll tell him you were asking about him."

Gordon let himself in and went directly to the side

window. When the lights went on inside Shirley's house, he went back outside and fetched the case of beer from the car. He cracked one open as soon as he was back inside and put the rest in the refrigerator. He took a small plate from the kitchen to use as an ashtray and turned on the TV in the living room. He lit a cigarette and settled onto the sofa with his beer just as the final round of Wheel of Fortune began. The normalcy of it all set him at ease, and Gordon realized he could easily get used to living this way. He had everything he needed—and some.

After his second cigarette and third beer, Gordon started taking his belongings upstairs. There were two bedrooms on the second floor: Uncle Milton's old bedroom and a guest room that hadn't been used for ages. Gordon set himself up in the guest room, having no desire to sleep in the bed that had once been used by his uncle.

Dead uncle.

The only other room on the second floor was a small bathroom located at the top of the stairs. Gordon arranged his limited supply of toiletries around the sink and on the back of the toilet. He began unpacking the clothes that had been unceremoniously stuffed into garbage bags by Mr. Crutch, then decided to wash them before putting them away in the dresser. He carried one bag of clothes downstairs, loaded them into the washing machine, and started the cycle. He grabbed another beer from the fridge and nearly dropped it when he heard a muffled banging sound from the other side of the cellar door.

What the hell was that?

Gordon stared at the door for a full minute, waiting to see if the sound came again. When it did not, he pressed his ear against the door and heard what sounded like a faint groaning sound. The legs of a chair squealed on the linoleum as Gordon backed into it. He continued retreating away from the door until his hip struck the counter. He remembered the beer in his hand and gulped down half of it with his eyes still glued to the cellar door.

What the hell was that? He can't still be alive. Can he?

Gordon considered the possibility. He had never checked to confirm that his uncle was dead before throwing him into the cellar—at least, he had no memory of doing so.

He can't be alive.

Gordon reasoned that even if the blow to the head from the pickle jar hadn't killed him, the fall down the stairs would have done the job.

Wouldn't it?

This line of thinking conjured the image of Uncle Milton's body lying in darkness at the foot of the stairs. He felt his nerves tighten, and his hands began to shake. Everything he had said and done to convince himself that this was a manageable situation vanished in an instant, replaced by panic.

If he's not dead, he's dying now.

Gordon went into the living room and lit a cigarette. A happy jingle advertising some kind of drug played on the TV while a friendly voice listed potentially harmful side effects. The television once again reminded him that the rest of the world was carrying on as if nothing had happened, completely ignorant of what he had done.

No one knows.

The simplicity of that statement and its implications helped to settle Gordon's nerves.

No one will know if you don't tell them, he assured himself. *You've done this before.*

A long-buried memory began to push its way to the surface of Gordon's mind like a reanimated corpse rising from its grave.

Simpleton.

Despite the unsettling nature of that memory, Gordon was reminded that he had successfully kept that secret for his entire adult life. He could do it again.

No one knows.

Gordon finished his beer, returned to the kitchen, and gently set the empty can down on the counter. He realized that he was trying to be quiet so as not to be heard by Uncle Milton, if he was, in fact, still alive.

If he's not dead, he will be soon. Gordon let the thought settle in. *He can't live without food or water. Or his medicine.*

Gordon walked quietly past the bathroom and into Uncle Milton's bedroom. He knew his uncle took pills every day because he often picked them up at the pharmacy for him, but he had no idea what they were for. He looked at one of the pill bottles on the dresser, squinting at the small print. He couldn't pronounce the name on the label and didn't bother to read further. Gordon pondered how crucial they were and whether his uncle would survive without them, but he had no way of knowing. He returned to the kitchen and stared at the door.

He must be dead.

Gordon opened the refrigerator and grabbed another beer.

You can always check to be sure.

The thought of opening the cellar door made Gordon's stomach turn. Seeing his dead uncle down there would be bad enough, but seeing him alive would be even worse. "I am not opening that door," Gordon whispered to himself. "Ever."

Gordon grabbed a second beer from the fridge and carried both upstairs. He closed the bedroom door and retrieved a pair of sweatpants from one of the remaining bags of clothes. He chugged one of the beers and set the other on the nightstand beside the bed. He suddenly felt very tired and got under the covers. He turned off the light and fell asleep within minutes.

Gordon opened his eyes in the dark room, unsure of what had awakened him. He heard a clanky, banging sound from somewhere else in the house and realized that the repetitive thumping was what had stirred him from sleep. He initially assumed the old heating system was to blame, but the sound had a rattling quality to it, unlike the typical ticking and tapping caused by hot water moving through the pipes and radiators. After listening for a full minute, Gordon got out of bed and went to the bedroom door. The sound became louder upon opening the door, and his attention was immediately drawn to the stairs. The living room below was dimly lit by the glow of the streetlight filtering through the sheer curtains of the front window. Uncle Milton's empty wheelchair sat at the foot of the stairs, the footrest touching the lip of the bottom step. As Gordon watched, the wheelchair rolled backward a couple of inches before lurching forward. The metal footrest banged into the bottom step, causing the chair to shudder and rattle. Gordon clutched the doorframe as he watched the process repeat twice more before retreating into the bedroom and slamming the door shut. He slapped the light switch on the wall beside the door, but it was already in the on position. He hurried over to the bedside lamp and turned it on, filling the room with light. Turning back to the door, Gordon searched the room for a way to secure it. The door had no lock, so he pushed the dresser in front of it, its feet groaning loudly as it slid across the wooden floorboards. Gordon held his breath, staring at the barricaded door as he waited for the sound to come again, but the house had fallen still. His shirt was damp with sweat, and he suddenly felt very cold. He grabbed the blanket that was folded at the foot of the bed and wrapped it around his shoulders. He sat on the bed and noticed that one of the two beer cans on the nightstand remained unopened. He popped the tab and took several gulps of the warm beer. The floor was cold under his bare feet, so he repositioned himself with his back against the headboard and drew his legs up under the covers. He kept the light on while nursing his beer, eyes fixed on the barricaded door, ears tuned to every little sound. The house was mostly quiet, but just before he dozed off, Gordon thought he heard soft scratching behind the walls.

18

Sunlight sliced into the room through a gap at the bottom of the window blinds. Gordon stared at the sliver of light as he slowly came awake. He sat up in bed, and a mostly empty beer can rolled off the blanket and clunked onto the floor. He noticed the dresser in front of the door and, an instant later, remembered what had happened in the middle of the night. If the door had not been barricaded, he might have thought the wheelchair incident was just a bad dream.

Gordon went to the window and opened the blinds, allowing the gray morning light to fill the room. A car drove down the block, and a man walked up the steps of the house across the street with a folded newspaper in his hand. All was well in the outside world; it was just another ordinary day. The scene unfolding in broad daylight made the wheelchair incident seem much less plausible. The notion that it had been a dream, or at least something other than what he had initially thought, started to sound much more plausible to Gordon. He turned his attention to the door. *There's only one way to know for sure,* he thought, moving to the dresser and sliding it back into place to the right of the door. He took a deep breath, opened the door, and looked downstairs.

There was no wheelchair at the foot of the stairs.

Gordon sighed with relief and started down the stairs, gradually taking in the living room as more of it came into view. All appeared as it had the night before. He headed for the kitchen, collecting empty beer cans from the coffee table as he passed it by. He dropped the cans in the trash and peeked into Uncle Milton's bedroom before turning into the bathroom. The wheelchair was there, parked beside the bed, exactly where he'd left it. After relieving himself, Gordon splashed some cold water on his face and regarded his reflection in the mirror over the sink. Dark bags hung under his eyes, and several days of beard stubble lined his jaw. He ran his damp hands over his scalp, smoothing out his thinning hair. He cupped a handful of water to his mouth, rinsed, and spat it out into the sink. Feeling somewhat refreshed, Gordon returned to the kitchen and froze in his tracks.

The cellar door stood open.

It was only partway open, but it was enough to send a chill racing up Gordon's spine. He immediately pushed it closed, but the latch didn't fully set in the strike plate, and the door fell open as soon as he withdrew his hand. He pushed hard against it with both hands until he heard the latch click into place, and then he stepped away. He reminded himself that the doors in the old house occasionally did that, but he still felt unnerved. He slid one of the chairs from the kitchen table in front of the door for good measure, then went in search of his cigarettes. He found the half-empty pack in the living room and immediately lit one up. He switched on the TV but paid little attention to what was on. His mind kept drifting back to what had happened in the middle of the night, trying to convince himself that it had indeed been a dream.

But the dresser had been pushed in front of the door, he reminded himself. *That was no dream.*

Determined to silence his doubts, Gordon allowed his inner voice of reason to take center stage.

There was no wheelchair at the foot of the stairs this morning, it said. *It had never been there. It had to have been a dream because what you saw—what you think you saw—is impossible.*

What if it rolled back into the bedroom on its own? Gordon argued, despite his desire to believe the voice of reason.

Things like that don't happen in real life. You know this. Don't be stupid.

Gordon decided to inspect the bottom step for signs of damage. If the wheelchair *had* been banging against it, it would have left visible marks. Kneeling in front of the step, Gordon ran his fingers over the beveled lip of the stair and felt several grooves in the wood.

Those marks could have been there for years, the voice of reason declared. *It doesn't prove anything.*

Though not entirely convinced, Gordon decided to accept that conclusion. He stood and returned to the kitchen, his eyes immediately drawn to the cellar door. The door remained closed with the chair against it. He poured himself a glass of milk and scanned the countertops for something to eat. Nothing appealed to him, so he decided to go out for breakfast. He wanted to get out of the house anyway.

The nightmare teased at the back of his mind as he ate his Egg McMuffin and hash browns, but he was beginning to accept that it had, in fact, been a dream. He gazed out the window at the bank next door and considered the cash that was now available to him. There wasn't enough money in the account to pay for anything significant, but Uncle Milton received pension payments every month, and there was no reason why those should stop coming. As long as everyone believed Uncle Milton was still alive, the deposits would continue to land in the account.

Gordon rarely thought about the future. He rarely thought about anything beyond the end of the workweek and when he would have his next drink. The unforeseeable future was full of uncertainty, and long-term plans required commitment and responsibility—two things that Gordon strove to avoid. But now, with the possibility of some decent income, he might be able to do something different, something better. He knew he couldn't maintain the charade indefinitely, so he needed to come up with an endgame of sorts—an escape plan. He would have to relocate and start anew somewhere else. He needed to save up a good amount of cash, drive away, and never look back. He imagined himself living in another state and renting a nice little place of his own. Someone would eventually find Uncle Milton in the abandoned house, but he'd be long gone by then. He would just have to keep a low profile. If anyone ever did catch up to him, he would just have to play dumb and say he knew nothing about Uncle Milton's demise. He would say it must have happened after he'd left.

No one will believe that.

Gordon tried to ignore the voice of reason. His plan was far from complete, but at least it was a start. He would continue to work it out, and things would eventually fall into place. For now, he had a roof over his head and some spending money.

But will the pension checks be enough?

Uncle Milton was not rich, and the bank account would not cover much more than the monthly bills that were sure to come. Gordon began to wonder if his uncle had more money stashed away somewhere: in another account or possibly hidden somewhere in the house. There might even be some valuables that he could sell.

Feeling motivated, Gordon headed home to see what he could find, stopping at the liquor store along the way.

19

Gordon sipped his rum and Coke with his feet up on the coffee table. It had been a relatively busy day, and he felt he deserved a good rest and a nice cocktail. While searching Uncle Milton's desk, he had found a passbook for a savings account with a couple of thousand dollars in it, but it was not nearly enough to fund Gordon's future, even if he was able to access the account. He thought the POA might allow him to do it, but he wasn't willing to attempt it at this early stage, especially since it might draw unwanted attention. His search of the desk yielded a few other items he thought he could sell for cash. He found a tin box filled with old coins and knew they were worth their weight in silver at the very least. He had also found several old foreign currency bills and hoped that they, too, might be worth something. He searched all the drawers in Uncle Milton's old upstairs bedroom and checked the pockets of his suits hanging in the closet for cash, but found nothing of value there. He searched every place in the house he could think of except for the cellar, but there was no way he was going down there—ever.

Gordon opened his eyes to find the ten o'clock news

on the TV. He had fallen asleep while sitting up on the sofa and had developed a painful kink in his neck. He picked up the glass from the side table and grimaced at the taste of flat, watered-down soda and rum. It was nearly eleven o'clock on a Sunday night, but he decided to make himself a fresh drink since he didn't have to get up for work the next morning. While it was initially appealing, the thought of being unemployed did not sit well with him. It forced him to kill time during the day and lie to his friends at Cormack's. It also made him entirely dependent on Uncle Milton's resources, which were shaping up to be a break-even situation. If he had some income of his own, he could save everything he earned and use those funds to start his new life, whatever that might turn out to be. But who would hire a fifty-nine-year-old man who had been fired for drinking on the job?

You weren't exactly fired, the voice of reason piped in. *You can get your old job back if you complete the program.*

Gordon winced at the idea. The last thing he wanted to do was to quit drinking. It was his favorite pastime, the thing he most looked forward to every day. He loved his beer, and the shots, and his rum and Coke. He couldn't imagine never going to Cormack's again. All his friends were there.

Maybe I could fake it, Gordon thought, weighing the idea. *I could attend the meetings and pretend to stop drinking. Then Kate and Suski would have to take me back.*

Gordon winced again. He knew he wouldn't be able to fool those AA people—not without opening up about his past and discussing his reasons for drinking.

Simpleton.

"Nope. Not doing that," Gordon said out loud, dismissing the idea once and for all. He grabbed the remote and started scrolling through the channels. He still had plenty of rum and could stay up as late as he wanted.

Gordon woke up in the upstairs bedroom. He was still fully dressed, save for his shoes. He didn't remember coming upstairs or getting into bed. He'd been drawn from sleep by the need to urinate and switched on the bedside lamp before getting up to use the bathroom. After flushing the toilet, Gordon heard a clatter from downstairs. Stepping out of the bathroom, he looked down into the living room.

Uncle Milton's wheelchair was there, at the foot of the stairs.

Gordon watched dumbstruck as the wheels on one side rose off the floor an inch or two before dropping back down as the opposite side lifted into the air. It repeated the process, swaying from side to side at an increasing speed. The chair rattled and clanked, violently pitching back and forth. Gordon's entire body tingled as if his blood had been replaced with ice water. He tore his eyes from the impossible sight and practically dove into the bedroom. The small rug on the landing at the top of the stairs slipped out from beneath his feet, causing him to tumble through the doorway. His forehead struck the doorknob as he went down, and white light exploded in his head. He rolled onto his knees, wincing and cursing as he kicked the door closed. Pain eclipsed the fear that had caused him to slip and fall, replacing it with anger. He pushed himself off the floor and climbed into the bed. He covered his head with a pillow, holding it in place with one arm. The pillow covered his ears, muting all sound save for his own breathing, and he was soon fast asleep.

20

Rain thrummed on the roof and lashed against the window. Gordon opened his eyes and then closed them again, repeating the process several times before finally sitting up in bed. His head hurt, but not in the way it so often did upon waking. He brushed his fingers across his forehead and sucked in a breath when they touched the sensitive spot. He checked himself in the mirror over the dresser and found his forehead bruised with a small scab in the center of the raised area.

Pulling open the bedroom door, Gordon noticed the rug bunched up against the door of Uncle Milton's old bedroom on the opposite side of the small landing. He remembered slipping on the rug and the frightening sight that made him want to flee into the bedroom. He immediately looked downstairs but was not surprised to see no wheelchair waiting below. He couldn't rationalize what he had seen—or thought he had seen —and saw no reason to try, having failed to properly explain the first occurrence. It had to have been a dream, or the product of an overactive imagination.

Or a ghost.

Dismissing the thought, Gordon turned into the bathroom. He brushed his teeth and noticed blood mingling with the toothpaste when he spat into the sink. His teeth ached when he rinsed, and one tooth in particular reacted to the cold water with an electric jolt. Gordon hadn't visited a dentist in years, and knowing he needed dental work only made him want to put it off even more. He gently cleaned the wound on his forehead, then went back to the bedroom, where he pulled on a pair of jeans and a clean T-shirt. He went downstairs and found the living room just as he'd left it the night before. Thunder rumbled as he entered the kitchen, and Gordon froze in place.

The cellar door was slightly ajar.

The chair he had positioned in front of the door prevented it from opening more than a few inches, but anything was too much for Gordon. He took one long step forward and pushed the door closed, leaning against it until the latch clicked into place.

Had the chair not been directly against the door? he wondered. *I thought it was. Is it possible that it opened with enough force to move the chair?*

Gordon replaced the chair, this time ensuring it was positioned firmly against the door. As he turned around, he saw the handles of Uncle Milton's wheelchair poking out of the bathroom doorway.

"What the hell?"

Gordon approached slowly, fearing he might find his uncle's lifeless body slumped in the chair, but he found the chair empty, prompting a sigh of relief. He tried to remember if he had left the wheelchair there. He had moved it out of the way a couple of times while searching Uncle Milton's room the day before, but he did not specifically remember parking it in the bathroom.

You must have, said the voice of reason. *It's the only logical explanation.*

Gordon wanted to believe that, but he also wanted to be rid of the wheelchair once and for all. At least then, he would no longer have to worry about it rolling around the house at night. He considered folding the wheelchair and storing it somewhere, but he didn't think any of the closets were large enough to accommodate it. His eyes roamed over the kitchen and settled on the cellar door. Tossing the wheelchair down the cellar stairs seemed like the perfect solution, and he wondered why he hadn't thought of that when he dumped Uncle Milton's body down the stairs.

You did, but it wouldn't fit through the door.

Gordon vaguely remembered trying to push the wheelchair through the opening when Uncle Milton was still in it. The memory made him cringe and groan out loud. Still, he decided the cellar was the best place to dispose of the wheelchair. Maybe, after Gordon was long gone, when they discovered the body in the cellar, they would overlook the cellar door being too narrow and just assume that Uncle Milton had rolled through the open doorway by accident. If they did check the dimensions, things would be no worse than they already were, and Gordon wouldn't be around to answer any questions anyway.

With his mind made up, Gordon rolled the wheelchair into the kitchen. He moved the kitchen chair aside, then paused before turning the doorknob. His mouth felt suddenly dry.

I don't want to see him down there!

He grabbed a glass and went to the sink for a drink of water, but instead reached for the bottle of rum on the counter. He unscrewed the cap and poured two fingers into the glass. He gazed idly at the label as the liquor warmed his gut. Captain Morgan stood proud and confident with his boot on a barrel. Gordon imagined the stereotypical voice of a pirate saying, *"Argh! Don't be a coward, Boy!"* He took a second gulp of rum, set the empty glass on the counter, and strode to the cellar door. He pushed the chair aside and was greeted by a foul odor the moment he opened the door. *"Turn on the light!"* Captain Morgan commanded. *"Confirm the man is dead where ye left him!"* Gordon flicked the wall switch before his courage left him and immediately regretted the decision.

Uncle Milton stared up at him from down below.

Thunder pealed as if on cue.

"Holy shit!" Gordon swore, backing away from the open door and stumbling into the kitchen table. "That's not how he was!"

The last image of his uncle was seared into Gordon's memory, and it was not what he now saw. Uncle Milton had been lying on his side on the floor at the foot of the stairs, but now he was sitting up with his back against the wall.

But he's dead, right?

Gordon stepped forward and forced himself to take a hard look. His uncle's eyes were open but unfocused. Gordon stomped his foot hard on the floor, but Uncle Milton did not react. He called out once, and then a second time, much louder. Uncle Milton remained motionless, and Gordon was convinced.

He's dead alright.

Gordon grabbed the wheelchair by the handles and tried to force it through the opening, but as expected, it was too wide. He tossed the seat cushion through the doorway and watched it bounce off a step before disappearing over the side of the stairs. He pulled up on the handle in the center of the seat, and the wheelchair folded inward. He lifted it with both hands and threw it into the cellar. The wheelchair clanked and clattered as it cartwheeled down the stairs, coming to rest in a heap beside Uncle Milton's corpse. Gordon swatted the light switch, and the cellar went dark. He slammed the door shut, and when it refused to stay closed, he went to the junk drawer and grabbed a hammer and a small box filled with a variety of nails and screws. He leaned into the door and hammered two of the largest nails into the frame at an angle.

Once the door was secured, Gordon stepped back to assess his handiwork.

"Now try to open," he dared the door.

Setting the hammer down on the table, Gordon leaned against the counter and waited for his breathing and heart rate to slow. The foul smell still hung in the air, so he opened the window over the sink to let some fresh air in. The outside air was damp, but not unbearably cold. He reached for the rum and poured the remainder into the glass. He thought he saw Captain Morgan wink at him just before tossing the empty bottle into the garbage bin.

21

"Do you believe in ghosts?"

One of Mack's eyebrows rose in response to the unexpected question.

"I guess that's a no, then," Gordon said, picking up his beer and taking a sip.

"I generally don't respond to questions that include the word 'believe,'" Mack said. "It usually leads to trouble."

"I'm just curious, that's all. I'm not judging or anything."

"I've never seen a ghost if that's what you're getting at," Mack said, crossing his arms over his chest. "Have you?"

Gordon shrugged. "I don't know. Maybe."

"Okay. I'll bite," Mack said. He waved a hand at the row of empty barstools. "I got time."

Gordon suddenly realized he didn't want to describe what he had seen—or thought he had seen. "Nothin', really," he said after a thoughtful pause. "Like I said, I was just curious."

"Aw, come on," Mack goaded. "You can't tease me like that. You obviously thought you saw something. What was it? Did you see something in your uncle's house? You're still living there, right?"

"Yeah, I'm all moved in. I've just been hearing weird noises at night, that's all."

"What kind of noises?"

"I don't know, like, banging sounds downstairs while I'm upstairs in the bedroom," Gordon said, idly scratching the label on the bottle with his thumbnail.

"How do you know it's not your uncle?" Mack asked. "Maybe he's getting up in the night."

A chill ran up Gordon's spine, and he looked up at Mack before nervously averting his eyes. "I don't think so."

"Well, did you ask him? You must have asked him."

"Yeah, I asked him," Gordon lied. "He said it's probably the radiators making the noises."

"Well, that makes sense," Mack said. "We had radiators in the house I grew up in. They made all kinds of racket on winter nights. That's probably your ghost."

Both men turned as Remmy walked into the bar. He settled onto the stool next to Gordon while Mack fetched him a beer from the cooler.

"How about you?" Mack asked, placing the beer in front of Remmy. "Do you believe in ghosts?"

"What'd I miss?" Remmy asked, reaching for his beer.

"Gordon here thinks his uncle's house is haunted," Mack said with a grin.

Remmy sat up straighter in his seat. "Really?"

"I never said that," Gordon contested. "I just heard some noises, that's all."

"Ghosts are real alright," Remmy said. "My niece's house is totally haunted."

"Do tell," Mack said, assuming his usual crossed-arms stance behind the bar.

"Well, things were gettin' moved around at night, and sometimes they would find the kitchen cabinets open in the morning." Remmy's tone grew increasingly serious as he spoke. "One time, when I was there for a family thing, we heard a crash in the kitchen. We all ran in there and found a broken glass on the floor. No one was in the kitchen. It happened all by itself."

"Really?" Gordon asked, looking Remmy square in the eyes.

"Yep. My niece said the guy who lived there before them died in the house. They think it was him doing all that stuff."

Mack shook his head and retrieved a shot glass from the shelf behind him. He filled it with water from the sink and then poured it onto the bar, forming a small puddle. "Watch this," he said, placing the shot glass in the middle of the puddle. The glass remained still for a couple of seconds and then began to slide toward Mack. He caught the glass just as it slipped over the edge of the bar. "Happens all the time."

Remmy's face pinched into a scowl. "Yeah, well, this old dump ain't exactly level," he argued. "My niece had brand new granite counters installed."

Mack shrugged and was about to return the shot glass to the shelf when Gordon said, "You might as well fill that with somethin' besides water while you have it handy."

Remmy snorted. "Make it two."

To their surprise, Mack lined up three shot glasses on the bar.

"Ooh," Remmy exclaimed. "You're joining us?"

"Why not?" Mack said cheerfully, taking a bottle of chilled Jägermeister from the cooler and filling the glasses. "It's the holiday season. This round's on me."

All three men picked up their glasses.

"Here's to ghosts," Mack said before downing his shot.

"You shouldn't joke about that," Remmy said, shot still in hand.

Gordon didn't drink his either.

"Why's that?" Mack inquired. "Are they listening?"

"They might be," Remmy said, turning to Gordon and bobbing his shot in the air. "I got a better one. To the dead," he said. "May they rest in peace."

22

The house was completely dark when Gordon pulled into the driveway. It occurred to him that he should leave some lights on when he was out if he wanted others, especially Shirley, to believe that Uncle Milton was still alive and well. He walked to the front door with a bag of McDonald's in one hand and a twelve-pack in the other. A cat hissed and darted out from beneath the wheelchair ramp, causing Gordon to nearly trip over his own feet as he leaped back in surprise. The all-white cat paused to regard him from the corner of the porch, its eyes eerily capturing the light of the streetlamp. Gordon wanted to throw something at the animal, but his hands were full of things he did not want to part with. He stomped a foot on the metal ramp and growled like a dog, but the cat merely flinched and did not run away. Gordon ascended the steps beside the ramp and set the food and beer on the bench beside the front door. He grabbed a broom that was leaning against the wall, quietly stepped over to the corner of the porch, and swung it down where he had last seen the cat. There came another hiss, and a white blur shot to the driveway, where it stopped and arched its back in a classic Halloween cat pose. It glared back at Gordon, the fur on its back and tail standing on end.

"Don't fuck with me," Gordon warned the cat. "And tell your friends, too."

Gordon went inside and sat on the sofa with his fast food and beer spread out on the coffee table. He turned on the TV and quickly changed the channel when Jeopardy came on. That program would forever remind him of Uncle Milton shouting "Kalamazoo" at the TV. He settled on a sitcom rerun and idly watched as he alternated bites of burger and fries. He washed down his meal with a beer, and as he stood up to grab another, something small and brown darted along the bottom edge of the wall and into the kitchen. It looked like either a large mouse or a small rat. Gordon hurried to the doorway, but the rodent was out of sight by the time he stepped into the kitchen. He didn't think there was enough space for it to have slipped under the cellar door, which, thankfully, remained closed. Getting down on his knees, he scanned the perimeter along the floor and noticed a gap in one corner beneath the cabinets. He crawled closer and concluded that a mouse or rat could easily fit through the small opening. Brown stains marred the linoleum just outside the hole, and Gordon wondered what kind of foul crap the creatures were tracking around the house. He knee-walked to the corner cabinet where the cleaning supplies were kept and grabbed the first spray bottle he could find. He sprayed lemon-scented disinfectant into the hole until a small puddle formed on the floor. Satisfied with his temporary solution, Gordon returned to the living room with a fresh beer.

The coins he had found in Uncle Milton's desk the day before were still on the end table where he had left them. Seeing them prompted Gordon to look around for anything else of value that he might be able to sell. He didn't know much about antiques, but everything in the house was pretty old, and he thought some of the stuff might be worth something to somebody. He walked through the house, using his phone to take photos of the furniture, lamps, and knick-knacks, thinking he could show them to someone who could assess their value.

As he returned to the living room, his phone rang in his hand, and he tossed it away as if it were on fire. Gordon stared at the phone as it continued to ring several more times on the floor, making no move to pick it up. He circled around it and grabbed his beer from the coffee table. He sipped the beer until the phone made the sound indicating a message had been saved to voicemail. He picked up the phone and opened the voicemail app, but did not recognize the displayed number. He played the message, hoping it would be a telemarketer or a wrong number, but it turned out to be the garage calling about his car. The mechanic said there were several issues to address and asked him to return the call to discuss repairs and costs. Gordon sighed with relief, thankful that it wasn't Karen or Kate from HR calling. He returned to the sofa and settled in to watch an old movie he had seen several times before. By the time he went upstairs to bed, ten of the twelve beers he had bought were gone.

Gordon opened his eyes, roused by a full bladder. He didn't need to turn on the light because he had fallen asleep with the bedside lamp still on. Movement on the floor near the radiator under the window caught his eye as he sat up in bed. Surprise turned to anger when he realized what it was. It was most definitely a rat, for it was too big to be a mouse. Gordon despised rodents, and the thought of them living in the house irked him to his core. The rat regarded him, its whiskers twitching, and Gordon noticed that the fur around its nose and mouth was stained with a dark substance.

Is that blood?

Gordon wondered if the chemicals he'd sprayed into the hole had given the creature a bloody nose, but he couldn't be sure.

Had it been eating something that was already dead?

The thought of rats gnawing on Uncle Milton's body in the cellar flashed through Gordon's mind, and he sat up in a hurry. The sudden movement startled the rat, which quickly vanished through the gap where the radiator pipe passed through the floor. Cursing under his breath, Gordon went to the bathroom to relieve himself. He recalled the events of the past two nights and was relieved to see no wheelchair when he looked down the stairs.

At least there's that.

Gordon fell asleep with terrifying visions haunting his mind. Uncle Milton gazed up from the dark cellar, blood-red tears leaking from his eyes. Rats swarmed over his lifeless body, biting and gnawing.

23

Gordon stepped out into the chilly morning air. He zipped his winter coat all the way up as he walked to the car, pausing when he noticed a cat crouched beside the ground-level window on the side of the house. The cat, which he recognized as the one that had jumped out of the shed the week before, glanced briefly at Gordon before returning its attention to something beyond the glass. Gordon shivered, both from the cold and the unsettling awareness of what the cat was doing.

It's looking into the cellar.

Gordon walked around the passenger side of the car and shooed the cat away from the window. He knelt in the driveway, but the glare of the morning light on the glass made it difficult to see inside. Getting fully down on his knees, Gordon shaded his eyes and brought his face closer to the glass.

A pale face looked back at him.

Gordon fell backward onto his butt, the back of his head striking the Cadillac's front fender. He scrambled to his feet, never taking his eyes from the window.

Had that been Uncle Milton's face?

It was your own reflection, you idiot.

Gordon tried his best to believe the voice of reason as he got into the car. He decided it would be a good idea to cover that window, just to be safe. As unlikely as it may be, he didn't want to risk someone looking in and seeing Uncle Milton's corpse in the cellar. He was going to the hardware store anyway, so he mentally added plywood to his shopping list.

After withdrawing cash from the ATM, Gordon stopped at the 7-11, where he bought cookies, chocolate milk, and two packs of cigarettes. He ate his breakfast in the parking lot and then drove to the hardware store, where he purchased several rat traps, a box of nails, and a quarter-sheet of plywood. He smoked a cigarette in the liquor store parking lot while he waited for it to open, then bought a case of beer, a quart of rum, and a two-liter bottle of Coke. He returned home with his supplies and immediately went to work boarding up the cellar window.

Using a rusty handsaw he found in the shed, Gordon cut the plywood to the approximate size on the back steps. He aligned it over the window, intentionally trying to avoid looking through the glass. The board was larger than necessary, but he decided to use it as it was rather than making another cut. He hammered the first nail in, expecting it to bite into the wood around the window frame, but knew he had missed his mark when he heard glass shatter behind the plywood.

"Shit!"

"What on earth are you doing, Gordon?"

Gordon turned toward the sound of the voice and saw Shirley standing on the other side of the fence at the back of her house, holding a bag of dry cat food in one hand. Two cats waltzed around her legs as three more bounded into the yard from different directions.

"Uh, I'm trying to fix this window," Gordon said, still holding the board in place.

"What's wrong with it?"

"The glass broke, and cold air is getting in," Gordon said.

Shirley pointed her chin at the box containing Gordon's hardware purchases in the driveway. "You got a rat problem too?"

"Uh, yeah. I saw one last night."

"Well, I hope you're not putting any poison out," Shirley said. "I wouldn't want the cats getting into it."

Gordon hadn't considered using poison, but he filed the idea away in the back of his mind in case the traps didn't work as planned; cats be damned. "I didn't get any poison," he said. "Just traps."

"These cats are my babies," Shirley continued. "I'd hate to see anything happen to them. Especially poison. That's a terrible way to go."

The board suddenly shifted beneath Gordon's hand,

and he turned away from Shirley, hoping she didn't notice his panicked expression. *Had it been pushed from the other side?* Pressing his knee against the board to hold it in place, Gordon quickly grabbed another nail and started hammering it in an inch to the side of the first failed attempt.

"Move over, Snowball," he heard Shirley say over the sound of dry pellets pouring into a metal bowl. "Make room for the others."

The nail bit into something solid on the other side, and Gordon drove it all the way in. He repeated the process several times while Shirley rambled on, unsure if she was speaking to him or the cats. Satisfied with his handiwork, Gordon stood and dropped the hammer in the box of supplies.

"Well, I can't say it's pretty," Shirley said, looking over the fence at the oversized board nailed to the side of the house.

"As long as it gets the job done," Gordon said, picking up the box. "I'll fix it right when the weather warms up."

Shirley looked up to the window above Gordon's head. "How's Milton?" she asked. "I'm surprised he's not supervising from the window."

Gordon followed her gaze, nervously glancing up at the window, half expecting to see a pale face leering back at him. "He's been spending a lot of time in bed lately," he said. "He's still not feeling great."

Shirley didn't respond, and when Gordon looked at her, he saw a skeptical frown on her face. *Was she starting to become suspicious of him?*

"I guess I'll go set these traps now," he said, wishing to end the conversation. "I'll tell Uncle Milton you were asking about him."

Back inside the house, Gordon placed a rat trap outside the hole under the counter in the kitchen and another by the radiator in the upstairs bedroom. He had bought the simple snap-trap variety since they were the least expensive. The hardware store clerk said it wasn't necessary to bait the traps in high-traffic areas, so Gordon decided to try that method first. He could always bait them later.

With the morning's chores complete, Gordon decided to get some lunch. He gathered the coins and foreign currency he'd found in Uncle Milton's desk and checked to make sure Shirley was not outside before going out to the car. He didn't like her persistent inquiries about Uncle Milton and planned to steer clear of her as much as possible from now on.

After a quick lunch at Burger King, Gordon drove to a coin store that had been in business for as long as he could remember. He collected coins briefly as a kid, but ultimately spent them on junk food and candy. The old man behind the counter was the same proprietor he remembered from childhood. He wasn't interested in the currency, but he offered to pay Gordon the current rate for silver by weight, insisting that they held no special value as coins. Gordon wasn't sure if he believed him, but he accepted the offer and left with two hundred and twenty-five dollars in cash. He'd already spent more than half that amount on lunch, the hardware supplies, gas for the Caddy, and, of course, the beer and booze. At this rate, he was never going to save up enough to make his exit before Shirley or someone else discovered his dark secret. He needed to get his hands on more money. Much more. Until he figured out how to do that, he would have to control his spending. He decided to pick up some groceries at the store to save on food and forgo his daily visit to the bar. He would have to spend less time at Cormack's. He could save a lot by drinking at home.

Gordon had three boiled hot dogs with a side of potato chips for dinner. He put a significant dent in the beer supply while watching an old movie rerun, then dozed off on the sofa for a short time before going upstairs to bed.

"Kalamazoo!"

Gordon opened his eyes, unsure if he had heard the word or dreamed it. The cobwebs of sleep fell away, and he concluded that it had, in fact, been a dream, as it was the only logical explanation. He tried to recall the details of the dream but could only remember hearing Uncle Milton's voice, distant and muffled as if it were coming from downstairs.

And then a sound did come from downstairs.

It was a clinking metallic sound, one that Gordon's mind immediately associated with the familiar rattle of a doorknob. His eyes turned to the bedroom door, a faint rectangle in the gloom. He stared at the doorknob, fearing that it might start to rattle or, worse, turn. The distant clattering came again, followed by a muffled bang. Gordon held his breath to hear better, and three more loud reports broke the silence. In his mind's eye, he saw the cellar door; saw the old metal knob jittering as if being manipulated from the other side. He saw the wood vibrate as the banging came again, louder than before.

Gordon reached for the lamp too quickly and knocked it off the nightstand. He jumped out of bed, picked up the lamp, and switched it on before returning it to the nightstand. The lamp came on, bathing the room in cold light. Gordon went over to the door, listening for what might come next. More knocking sounds resounded throughout the house as if moving from room to room. A metallic clank from inside the room caused him to spin around and look toward the radiator beneath the window.

"It's the old heating system working overtime, you dope," Gordon muttered to himself. "It's freezing outside."

Gordon got back into bed and pulled the blankets up under his chin, grateful for the body heat they had retained. He switched off the lamp and closed his eyes. When the rattling sound came from just outside the bedroom door, he did his best to convince himself it was just the pipes.

24

Gordon had just walked into the kitchen when the wall phone rang, and he ducked as if something had been hurled at him. He stared at the phone as it continued to ring, willing it to stop. As soon as it did, his cell phone began ringing in the living room. He traced the sound to his coat and retrieved his phone from the inner pocket. He suspected it was Karen even before the display confirmed it.

"Hey Karen," Gordon said, trying to sound casual despite his rising anxiety.

"Gordy, have you seen Uncle Milton today?" she asked, getting straight to the point.

"Yeah, I'm at the house now."

"I just called. Why didn't you answer the phone?"

"Oh," Gordon said, realizing he should have thought of that. "That was you. I don't like answering his phone."

"Well, where is he? I want to talk to him."

"He's in the bathtub," Gordon said, resorting to one of the lies he had prepared in advance.

"Since when does he bathe in the morning?"

"He hasn't been feeling good, and wanted a hot bath, so I helped him."

"He's sick? What's wrong?"

"Don't worry, it's just a little cold, nothing major. I stayed over here the last couple of days to make sure he was alright."

"Has he seen a doctor?"

"He's fine. How's Nick doing?" Gordon asked, eager to change the subject.

"Oh, better than me, I suppose," Karen said, her tone more subdued.

"Is the medicine helping?"

"Medicine? You mean chemo?" Karen said, sounding annoyed once again.

"Yeah, that's what I meant."

"They started chemo two days ago. It's helping with the pain so far, but it's going to take a toll on him. I just know it."

"Is his hair gonna fall out?"

"Who the fuck cares about his hair, Gordy?" Karen snapped. "What the hell is wrong with you?"

"Sorry," Gordon said, feigning sincerity. "I just thought—"

"Just..." Karen paused, and Gordon felt sure she was chewing her lip. "Did you tell Uncle Milton what's going on? Because he hasn't called."

"Yeah, yeah, he knows. I don't think he wants to talk about it," Gordon said, fabricating the lie on the spot. "I could tell he was bothered by it, even though he didn't say much. I think because he's so old, he—"

"Just tell him to call me," Karen cut in.

Gordon didn't have to reply because his sister ended the call. He flopped down onto the sofa and released a heavy sigh. He wasn't sure how long he could put Karen off, not to mention Shirley. He was beginning to realize he wouldn't be able to maintain the charade as long as he had hoped.

A wave of anxiety rose from Gordon's gut. He knew his escape plan was severely underdeveloped and that he had been putting it off for too long. He'd been taking things day by day, hoping answers would fall into place, but time was running out. He would have to hit the road soon, but he had not seriously considered where he would go or what he would do once he got there. He thought he might be able to keep the lie going for another week or so, but not long beyond that. He lit a cigarette and kept the lighter's flame burning, briefly considering the idea of setting the house on fire and running out the door. *Maybe I will burn it down when I leave,* he mused. *Make them sift through the ashes to figure out what happened.*

The cigarette helped a little, but Gordon needed something more to settle his rising angst. He poured himself a rum and Coke, and the alcohol helped draw his thoughts away from the future and back to the more manageable present. "One day at a time," he muttered to himself, unaware of the irony of his words. "I just need to make a plan and stick to it."

Gordon fetched a pen and notepad from Uncle Milton's desk and sat down at the kitchen table. He realized he was facing the cellar door and moved to the chair on the other side of the table. He didn't like having his back to the door any better, so he took his drink and writing materials into the living room. He wrote the word "MONEY" on the first line of the notepad and then "PENSION" under that. Gordon glanced at the ever-growing mound of mail on the chair beside the front door, knowing it contained only junk and unpaid bills, with not a single check on the pile. Uncle Milton's checkbook ledger showed that the pension payments were directly deposited into the account on the first of every month, but January was still two weeks away, with Christmas falling in between. Gordon stared at the two words for a full minute before adding "SELL STUFF" to the list. He knew Karen would continue to be an ongoing problem, so he added her name to the list. He would need to have excuses prepared to explain Uncle Milton's inability to come to the phone, so he wrote "BATH," "BATHROOM," and "SLEEPING" under his sister's name. The excuses looked weak on paper, and Gordon knew they wouldn't hold up for long. He considered imitating his uncle's voice and thought he might be able to pull off a sick version of Uncle Milton over the phone. He added "FAKE IT" to the list and sank back into the sofa with a sigh. He glanced around the living room, looking for things he might be able to sell. He would need to find a pawn shop or antique dealer, which he also added to the list. He thought the old lamp on the side table might be worth something, despite its ugly appearance, so he decided to try to sell it first. He wrote "LAMP" on the line beneath "SELL STUFF," followed by "SMALL TABLE" and "LIVING ROOM CHAIR," both of which looked like antiques to Gordon's eye.

A door slammed outside, prompting Gordon to get up and look out the window facing Shirley's house. He watched her slowly descend the steps to where her son, Trey the Cop, was just getting out of his civilian car. They exchanged a few words that Gordon couldn't make out while Trey helped his mother into the passenger seat. After walking around to the driver's side, Trey looked directly at Uncle Milton's house before getting into the car. Something fluttered in Gordon's stomach, and he backed away from the window, hoping he had not been seen. He watched the car drive away, then added one more item to the list.

"SHIRLEY."

25

It was late afternoon when Gordon walked into Cormack's. He didn't want to return to the house, and since he had nowhere else to go, he decided to kill some time at the bar. He knew he was breaking his commitment to curb his spending, but he reassured himself that enjoying a couple of beers with friends wouldn't make much difference. His attempt to sell the antique lamp had been a complete waste of time and gas. He visited two different pawn shops in two different towns, but neither showed any interest in the lamp or any of the other items he had photographed with his cell phone. One suggested he try selling the items online, and the other advised him to donate them to Goodwill. Both said that no one was interested in antiques anymore.

Mack tossed a coaster onto the bar in front of Gordon and placed a Budweiser on it. Remmy walked in a moment later and sat down beside him.

"Hey, Gordy," he said. "Where have you been the last couple of days? Sick?"

"Nah, I've been busy taking care of my uncle and doing stuff around the house."

"How is old Milton?"

"He's seen better days." Gordon took a swig of beer. "Want to buy a lamp?" he prompted, hoping to change the subject.

"A lamp? What lamp?"

"Never mind," Gordon said, not wishing to discuss his failed mission either.

"You guys got any new ghost stories?" Mack asked, placing a fresh beer in front of Remmy.

"I could tell you more stuff that happened at my niece's place," Remmy offered.

"Let's hear it," Mack said, leaning back and crossing his arms.

"Well, my niece said she would sometimes hear voices," Remmy said, speaking in his most serious tone. "In addition to the usual banging around at night."

"And what, exactly, do ghosts talk about?" Mack asked, eyebrows raised in mock curiosity.

"I don't know," Remmy said, frowning. "They never told me."

"Is it still happening?" Gordon asked.

"I haven't been over there in a while, but I don't think so. They had someone come in and do stuff to get rid of the ghost. I think it worked."

"What kind of someone?" Gordon pressed, intrigued.

"Some spiritualist lady. I don't know what you call them. She came in with incense and walked around the house casting ghost-shooing spells or something." Remmy laughed. "I really don't know what she did, but like I said, I think it worked."

"How long ago was that?" Gordon asked.

"It was a while ago," Remmy said. "A year or more."

"Where did they find the lady?"

"Hell if I know," Remmy said, turning to look at Gordon. "Did something else happen at your uncle's place?"

"Yeah, how about it, Gordo?" Mack put in.

Gordon waved off the questions with the hand that wasn't lifting the beer to his lips. "No, no," he said. "I'm just curious, that's all."

"Maybe she's in the Yellow Pages," Mack quipped. "Under ghost exterminator."

Remmy laughed, and Gordon rolled his eyes. He didn't find it funny, but he didn't want his buddies to know that. "Do they still make Yellow Pages?"

Mack picked up his cellphone. "This is all you need," he said, deftly tapping the screen with his thumbs.

"I still have an old phone book on top of the fridge at home," Remmy said. "Can't remember the last time I used it, though."

"Here you go," Mack said without looking up from his phone. "There's a whole list of stuff you can do to get rid of unwanted spirits."

"Oh yeah?" Remmy said. "Like what?"

"It says to remove any items from your home that might contain negative energy," Mack said, a wry smile playing on his lips.

Gordon immediately thought of the wheelchair he'd thrown into the cellar. "How do you know if something has negative energy?"

"I'm just reading what it says here," Mack said. "It's all a bunch of crap."

"How did you find that?" Gordon asked.

"I just searched for 'How to get rid of a ghost,'" Mack said, putting the phone down on the counter behind him. "Do it yourself. You might even find a home course on exorcism and earn an online certificate."

Gordon forced a chuckle. He wanted to know more, but it would have to wait. For now, a round of shots was in order.

The smell struck Gordon the moment he walked through the front door. The rotten odor was more pungent in the kitchen, but it was not coming from the garbage bin. He checked the rat trap under the counter, thinking a dead rat might be responsible for the stink, but it had not been triggered. There was no rotting food or sour milk left out on the counter. He looked at the cellar door and remembered the bad smell he had noticed the last time he opened it. Though he was hesitant to confirm his growing suspicion, Gordon tested the air near the door. The offensive smell did seem stronger, and when he got down on his knees to sniff around the gap under the door, he immediately gagged. He withdrew from the door with his hand over his mouth and nose. The realization that he had been breathing air contaminated by a rotting corpse caused bile to rise from his gut. He got to his feet and hurried over to the sink, thinking he might be sick. He didn't vomit, but the foul odor lingered in his nostrils. He threw open the back door, stepped onto the stoop, and took several long breaths, relishing the cool, fresh air.

"Are you alright, Gordon?"

Gordon turned to find Shirley standing on her own back stoop, holding a bag of cat food.

"Yeah, I'm okay," he said, wiping his shirt sleeve across his chin.

"Well, you sure came outta there in a hurry," Shirley said, her face pinched in a scowl. "What's going on? Is Milton alright?"

"Yeah, he just..." Gordon stammered, struggling to come up with an excuse for his behavior. "I was... I had to clean up after him and needed some fresh air."

Shirley wrinkled her nose. "Oh, I see. I've been there myself, with my mother, before she died. It ain't easy caring for the elderly."

Gordon nodded, grateful that his quick thinking had

worked.

"Is he feeling any better?" she asked. "Have you called a doctor?"

"Yeah, I called," Gordon lied. "I told the doctor what was going on, and he told me what medicines to give him and all that."

The scowl returned to Shirley's face, and Gordon opened the storm door. "Well," he said, "I'd better get back to it."

"Have you tried chicken soup? Shirley asked. "I could make him some. Homemade."

"Oh, thanks, but that's okay. I got a bunch of cans in the house. I'll tell him you offered, though."

Gordon hurried back into the house before Shirley could respond. The rotten stench greeted him once again, and he pulled a towel down from the shelf above the dryer just inside the door. He dropped the towel on the floor in front of the cellar door and nudged it into place with his foot to cover the gap. After a moment of consideration, he fetched a second towel and placed it under the faucet. He opened the window above the sink a couple of inches as the towel soaked up the water and then swapped the wet one with the first, firmly pressing it against the bottom of the door. Satisfied with his temporary solution, Gordon grabbed a beer from the fridge and flopped onto the sofa. He turned on the TV, and when he started to doze off, he went upstairs to bed.

Gordon descended the stairs in a daze. The streetlight outside seemed dimmer than usual, its weak light barely illuminating the living room. A knock came at the door, and he realized that the sound was what had drawn him out of his bedroom. He opened the door to find Shirley standing on the front porch. He knew it was odd for her to be calling in the middle of the night, but for some reason, he did not question it.

"I'm here to check up on Uncle Milton," she said. "I know you're up to something, Gordon. What did you do?"

"I don't know what happened," Gordon heard himself say. "I didn't do anything."

"I'm coming in," Shirley said, pushing Gordon aside.

Gordon attempted to block her with his body, and when that failed, he reached for her arm but suddenly felt weak and was unable to grab hold of her. He could only watch as Shirley marched into the dimly lit room.

"Uncle Milton," she said in a sing-song voice. "Where are you?"

A series of creaks echoed from the kitchen, and Gordon knew it was the sound of someone ascending the cellar stairs. He looked past Shirley to the kitchen doorway, a sense of dread building with every passing second. There came a loud bang, like a door being struck, and a shadow moved along the far wall of the kitchen. Uncle Milton stepped into the doorway, and despite the poor lighting, Gordon clearly saw his features. His face was pocked with red holes he somehow knew had been caused by biting rats. Bloody holes gaped where his eyes should have been.

"Why, Uncle Milton," Shirley exclaimed. "You're walking again!"

Gordon wanted to turn and run out the door, but he found himself unable to move. Uncle Milton turned his black eye sockets on Gordon, looking past Shirley, who also turned around to look at him. They both smiled.

"I guess everything's alright then," Shirley said, still smiling.

Uncle Milton began walking toward Gordon at an alarming speed. He passed right through Shirley, arms outstretched like Frankenstein's monster. His jaw fell open, and blood dribbled down his chin as he uttered a single word.

"Kalamazoo!"

A snapping sound drew Gordon out of the nightmare, and he immediately sat up in bed. The clattering persisted as he reached for the lamp and switched it on. Turning to the source of the noise, he saw a rat thrashing in the trap on the floor. The rodent eventually stilled, but Gordon remained unsettled by the dream that lingered so vividly in his mind. Try as he might, he could not shake the image of Uncle Milton's eyeless face.

26

Gordon felt the chill as soon as he entered the kitchen. The window had been left open overnight, but he didn't close it right away. He had to dispose of the rat first. He had dropped the dead rat into a small garbage pail after releasing it from the trap, which he then reset by the radiator in the upstairs bedroom. He carried the pail out through the back door, glanced around to see if anyone was watching, then flung the carcass over the fence at the back end of the yard. He returned to the kitchen, closed the window over the sink, and began washing his hands. Dealing with the dead rat had left him feeling unclean.

"Fucking things are disgusting," he muttered, drying his hands with a wad of paper towels.

The open window seemed to have cleared the terrible odor from the room, at least temporarily, yet it still lingered in his olfactory memory. Having no desire to experience it again, Gordon decided to take some preventative measures. He fetched a roll of duct tape from the junk drawer and tore off a long strip, which he stretched over the narrow gap at the top of the cellar door. He repeated the process until both sides of the door were also sealed with tape. He thought the towel was still the best solution for the larger gap at the bottom of the door, so he left it where it was. He knelt down to ensure it was still damp and noticed a dark shape under the counter where he'd placed the other trap.

Another rat.

The rat was dead, its head crushed in the trap just like the other one. He also noticed that this rat, like the first, had blood on its snout, which reminded him of his recent nightmares. As before, Gordon hoped that the blood was a result of the trap rather than remnants of what it had been eating. He picked up the trap, pulled back the trap bar, and let the rat drop into the pail. He disposed of the carcass just as he had the other and returned to the sink to wash his hands again.

"The place must be infested," he muttered. "Maybe I *should* try poison."

As he washed his hands, Gordon was reminded that it had been several days since he last showered, mainly because he didn't want to use the downstairs bathroom. The handicap conversions and wheelchair-accessible shower made it impossible not to think of Uncle Milton, but, like so many other things, it could only be avoided for so long. He showered quickly, then went upstairs to shave. Standing before the mirror, Gordon realized that he had the beginnings of a beard. It was mostly gray, and he thought it made him look older than he actually was. The disposable razor snagged and pinched as he shaved, resulting in several nicks on his chin and neck by the time he finished.

Feeling more refreshed than he had in days, Gordon went downstairs to have his breakfast. He pushed aside the beer cans and the saucer that served as an ashtray to make room for his cookies and chocolate milk on the coffee table. He turned on the TV and sat down at his regular dining spot. He ate more than usual, having bought an entire box of cookies rather than the individually wrapped packages he was used to. The early morning news was on, reminding Gordon that it was still very early. He had been unable to fall back asleep after the nightmare and the rat thrashing in the trap. The idea that rats might be consuming his uncle's corpse was certainly unsettling, but it wasn't the most troubling part of the dream. The very real possibility that Shirley might come knocking at the door at any moment was what worried him the most. Gordon felt sure she was beginning to suspect something was amiss, and he was running out of excuses. The thought of her showing up on the front porch filled him with dread.

After dozing off on the sofa for a while, Gordon got up and took the box of cookies and the empty glass into the kitchen. He heard Shirley's voice outside and looked out the vestibule window to see who she was talking to. She stood on the small concrete landing at the back of her house, picking up one of the metal dishes she had left out for the cats. He could hear her muffled voice through the glass pane.

"Your water is all frozen," she said, turning the bowl upside down and dumping a disk-shaped block of ice over the side of the stoop. "Y'all must be freezing out here."

Two cats paced back and forth at the bottom of the brick steps as if performing a rehearsed dance. Another came from behind the shed in Uncle Milton's backyard, jumping onto the fence before landing on Shirley's side.

"Oh, Lord, what is that?" Shirley cried, looking at something on one of the steps. "One of y'all brought me a present, huh? That's mighty nice, but I'm not fond of rats, thank you."

Shirley went inside and returned a moment later wearing yellow rubber gloves that reached up to her elbows. She picked up the dead rat, which Gordon presumed to be one of the two he had tossed over the fence, and carried it to a trash can at the end of her driveway on the opposite side of her property. She lifted the lid and dropped it in, grimacing. She went inside once more and returned with a bowl filled with water, some of which splashed out as she set it down on the stoop.

"I hope that doesn't freeze," she said. "I'm bound to break something if I slip and fall out here."

Shirley continued to talk to the cats as she poured dry cat food into a separate bowl, but Gordon was no longer listening. She had planted the seed of an idea in his brain, and it was already beginning to take root.

27

Gordon hurried back into the house after a quick trip to the 7-11 for cigarettes. A cold wind whipped at his heels, but the fresh air that followed him inside did little to alleviate the odor he noticed upon closing the door. Gordon thought about dead animals he had seen on the side of the road in the past and how they decomposed over time, concluding that the process didn't take very long. *But how long does it take for a human corpse to rot away and wither?* he wondered. *How long will I have to put up with this stench?*

The thought made Gordon feel nauseous. He was usually very good at keeping unwanted thoughts at bay, but that would be impossible as long as the house smelled like a morgue. He knew something had to be done about the worsening smell, but was unsure what to do. He considered air fresheners and burning incense, but that would only temporarily mask the smell. He needed a more permanent solution. He knew that covering or wrapping the body in something would help, but Gordon couldn't even consider the idea of going into the cellar, let alone handling Uncle Milton's corpse.

So, what then? What do I do?

Gordon opened the kitchen cabinet where the cleaning supplies were kept and took out a can of Lysol. He sprayed disinfectant into the air, and although the fresh, chemical scent helped, it would not solve the problem. He scanned the shelf above the washer in the vestibule and spied a bottle of bleach next to the detergent. He poured some of the solution onto the towel at the bottom of the cellar door, and the strong, chlorine-like odor filled the room. It was the best result so far, but Gordon thought it would be even more effective if he could apply it directly at the source, which led him to wonder what effect bleach would have on a dead body. He thought it might speed up the decomposition process and help with the smell, but applying it would require going down into the cellar.

Or would it? What if there were a way to pour bleach onto the body without having to go down there?

Gordon walked into the living room and stood at the bottom of the stairs. The cellar stairs ran directly under the living room stairs, which meant that Uncle Milton's body lay directly under the place where he was standing. The vision that formed in his mind sent a chill down his spine, but it also reinforced the idea he had been considering.

"I'll drill through the floor and pour bleach down the hole," he said, pleased enough with the idea to say it out loud. "That will do the trick!"

The foul smell once again greeted Gordon as he returned from the store with several bottles of bleach and a brand-new electric drill. He had been unable to locate Uncle Milton's drill, eventually concluding that it was probably on the tool shelf in the cellar. He also bought some cans of foam sealant made specifically to keep rodents out. He'd been forced to withdraw more money from the bank, but the purchases were essential. He lined the bleach bottles up beside the stairs and unboxed the drill. He fitted the largest bit into the chuck and plugged the cord into the wall outlet. The floorboard proved more solid than he had anticipated, and he was forced to start the hole with a smaller drill bit. After upsizing the bit several times, Gordon successfully created a hole nearly one inch in diameter in the floor. He inserted a plastic funnel into the hole and began pouring the bleach. He could hear the liquid splashing down below and hoped it was hitting its mark. After emptying the whole gallon, Gordon decided to wait and see how well it worked before using more, thinking it might be more effective to apply the bleach in staggered intervals. He removed the funnel and looked around for something to cover the hole. He remembered seeing an old wine cork in the junk drawer, which proved to be a nice fit.

"Now for those nasty rats," he said, grabbing a can of sealant from the box of supplies and carrying it into the kitchen.

He decided to address the hole under the counter

first and got down on his knees. He removed the seal on the can and sprayed the foam directly into the hole. Gordon was shocked by how much the foam expanded, and it happened so quickly that he got some of the sticky stuff on his hand. He crawled around on the kitchen floor, sealing every gap he could find, no matter how small. When the first can was empty, he grabbed another and continued to spray the foam around the pipes under the radiators all throughout the house. By the time he was done, he had worked up a sweat and was ready for a break.

"Now it's time to celebrate!" he declared.

Gordon celebrated in the usual manner and was well past drunk when the upstairs light went out next door. He had been watching Shirley's house all evening. He had second-guessed his plan to ice her back stoop several times early on, that pesky inner voice arguing that it was foolish, immoral, and downright evil, but Gordon had long since drowned the voice of reason in a sea of alcohol. If his plan was evil, he reasoned it was a necessary evil. It was just a matter of time before Shirley came knocking with homemade chicken soup or a box of Christmas cookies for Uncle Milton. She would want to see him, or at least hear his voice, and that would be the end of it for Gordon. She would tell her son, Officer Trey, and the law would come crashing down on him. They would find Uncle Milton dead in the cellar and lock Gordon up for life. He would never get away; never have the chance for a fresh start somewhere else.

It has to be done.

Gordon wasn't even sure if his plan would work, but he didn't believe anyone would suspect him of foul play if it failed. The temperature had been below freezing for several days, so the presence of ice was to be expected. If Shirley saw the ice before stepping outside, there was no reason to suspect that Gordon had been responsible for creating the hazard. The same should hold true if she did step onto the back stoop and fall, as he hoped. Even then, Shirley's injuries could range from very minor to severe, but either way, he hoped it would keep her out of his hair for a while.

He assumed the last light to go out belonged to Shirley's bedroom, but he waited a little while longer to give her time to fall asleep. He drank another beer to pass the time and bolster his resolve, then opened the back door, grabbing the watering can he had filled hours before on his way out. The hinges on the storm door seemed to creak louder than usual in the cold night air. He ensured the door was closed tightly to prevent it from blowing in the wind, then descended the three steps into the backyard. After confirming that Shirley's house was fully dark, he walked down the driveway to where the fence separating the two properties ended and crossed to Shirley's side. He noticed that a thin layer of ice had already formed in the water bowl left out for the cats and grinned. *This is going to work,* he thought as he slowly poured water over the concrete slab and brick steps of the back stoop. He emptied the watering can and went back to the house to refill it at the kitchen sink. He opened a can of beer, concluding that the first coating of water should be frozen by the time he'd finished it. He rubbed his hands together to warm them as he waited in the dark kitchen. The beer went down quickly, so he decided to have another. As he closed the refrigerator door, something groaned in the cellar.

Gordon froze.

"What the fuck was that?" he whispered. He waited for the sound to come again, hoping it would reveal itself as a natural occurrence, but heard nothing. He tried to reassure himself that it was just the boiler or water running through the pipes making the noise, but he couldn't shake the image of Uncle Milton groaning at him from below.

Gordon popped the beer can and chugged half of it. He looked at the clock on the wall and, despite being unable to read it in the gloom, decided that enough time had passed for the water to have frozen. He grabbed the watering can and went outside, eager to be out of the kitchen and away from the cellar door. He ran a hand over the cement surface of Shirley's back stoop and felt a smooth layer of ice in several places. He repeated the process of pouring water over the cement landing, and as he turned to go, he saw a cat observing him from a corner of the backyard. Despite the darkness, Gordon was able to identify it as the white one, the one Shirley called Snowball. Resisting the urge to hurl the watering can at the animal,

Gordon hurried around the fence, feeling the cat's eyes on his back. He tripped as he climbed the back stairs, banging his knee hard on the lip of a brick step. He bit back the groan and the litany of curses that rose in his throat and hobbled into the house through the back door. He dropped the watering can in the kitchen sink, grabbing the half-empty beer off the counter on his way to the living room. He flopped down on the sofa, lit a cigarette, and put his injured leg up on the coffee table. He tilted his head back and closed his eyes. He had planned to hit the stoop with one more coating of water, but he was soon fast asleep.

Gordon's foot slipped off the coffee table and hit the floor with a thud. Pain erupted from his knee, which had swollen while he slept. He opened his eyes to find the faint light of early dawn outside the front window. An empty can rolled off the sofa and clattered onto the floor as he pushed himself into a sitting position, his hand pressing into a cushion soaked with beer. As he reached for the cigarettes and lighter on the coffee table, he noticed the remnants of a cigarette on the floor beside his foot, a long trail of ash, and a black smudge on the floorboard beside the partially burned filter. Any feeling of gratitude for not setting the house—and himself—on fire was overshadowed by the pain in his knee that intensified as he leaned over to pick it up.

Fragments of what had transpired the night before began to surface in his clouded mind, including the reason for his injury. The fall on the back steps reminded him of why he had been outside, and he remembered pouring water on Shirley's back steps. He felt a sinking sensation in his gut as the realization of what he had done struck him. *I really did it,* he thought, his throat suddenly going dry.

Gordon got up to get something to quench his thirst and cursed as he put weight on his injured leg. He limped into the kitchen and filled a glass with water at the sink. He heard a clattering bang outside, which he associated with the sound of a storm door banging against something. He glanced out the back door but saw the storm door securely in place. He heard a muffled cry.

"Help!"

Gordon rushed over to the vestibule window that looked out on the back part of Shirley's house. Her storm door was flapping in the wind, and Shirley lay on the ground at the bottom of her back steps, one hand waving in the air as she continued to call out for help.

28

Gordon went inside and sank onto the sofa. He tucked his hands under his legs to warm his fingers, which had grown numb from standing outside in the cold for so long. He had called 911 immediately after checking on Shirley's condition, and the first police officer arrived in under two minutes. After radioing for an ambulance, the officer covered Shirley with a wool blanket from her car. Trey arrived moments later in uniform, visibly on the brink of panic. Paramedics arrived next and, after asking a lot of questions, very carefully maneuvered Shirley's ample body onto a gurney. They loaded her into the ambulance, and everyone drove off, leaving Gordon standing alone in the cold. Several cats watched him from the back of Shirley's yard as he limped up the back steps.

Guilt teased at the back of Gordon's mind, but he easily ignored it. He lit a cigarette and switched on the television, eager for a distraction. He surfed past the morning news until he came across an old sitcom rerun and let himself get absorbed in the simple plot. He finished the half-eaten box of cookies and soon began to feel very tired. Lack of sleep and the morning's events had finally caught up to him. His knee throbbed painfully as he slowly climbed the stairs, using the banister for support. He lay down on the bed, kicked off his shoes, and pulled the blankets over his head.

It was late afternoon when Gordon awoke to see snow falling outside the window. He had always liked the snow, and he got out of bed with the eagerness of a child. His knee had stiffened while he slept, forcing him to limp to the window. The rooftops and tiny front yards across the street were dusted with a fresh layer of whiteness, but the snow had yet to stick to the road. After using the bathroom, Gordon began slowly descending the stairs but stopped before reaching the bottom.

The cork lay beside the exposed hole in the floor at the foot of the steps.

Gordon envisioned the cork being pushed up and out of the hole from below by Uncle Milton's bony finger before driving the thought and the accompanying image from his mind. *I must have kicked it out when I went upstairs,* he thought, feeling somewhat assured by his assumption. The air in the living room smelled faintly of bleach, but the odor it was meant to eliminate was also present. Gordon used the banister to help him sit down on the second step from the bottom. He picked up the funnel and one of the bottles of bleach he had left by the stairs, inserted the funnel into the hole, and slowly poured the entire gallon into the cellar. He listened to the liquid splashing on something below and once again envisioned the bleach raining down on Uncle Milton's corpse. This time, though, he pictured the body in an advanced state of decomposition, the chemical liquid having dissolved much of the flesh. Despite the horrific image it evoked, he hoped the bleach was achieving just that, and that the stench of decomposition would soon be eliminated for good.

After replacing the cork in the hole, Gordon went into the kitchen to find something to eat. He opened the refrigerator, glanced at the package of hot dogs, and then shut the door. He opened the freezer, but Uncle Milton's frozen dinners looked even less appealing than the hot dogs. What he wanted was a Big Mac and fries.

After putting on fresh clothes, Gordon grabbed his coat from the chair by the front door. He felt his cell phone inside his pocket as he slipped it on, then took it out to check if it was still charged. He saw it was down to eleven percent, but he also noticed two missed calls and two voice messages. One was from Karen, the other from the mechanic. He didn't listen to either of them.

Gordon cleared the snow from the Caddy, drove to the bank to get cash from the ATM, and then walked next door to McDonald's. As he ate, unwanted thoughts continuously clamored for attention, despite his efforts to ignore them. Thoughts of Shirley and dead Uncle Milton flew at him like balls in a batting cage. He swatted them away, only to have others take their place. Uncle Milton's bank account was shrinking instead of growing, and Gordon had yet to fully develop his escape plan. He was beginning to wonder whether the upcoming pension deposit would be sufficient to finance his getaway or if he would need to postpone it for another month. Shirley was out of the picture for the time being, but Gordon had no idea how long that would last. The unanswerable questions continued to pile up in his mind until it became unbearable. He needed to quiet his thoughts.

He needed a drink.

Cormack's was busier than usual, and Gordon had to ask a patron to slide over so he could sit next to Remmy.

"It's awfully crowded today, huh?" he said.

"Friday at quittin' time," Remmy said with a shrug. "Everybody wants to get their end-of-the-week buzz on."

Gordon nodded, realizing that he had completely lost track of what day it was.

"What's the matter with your leg?" Remmy asked, having noticed Gordon's limp.

"I slipped on the steps and banged my knee," Gordon said, his eyes on Mack, who was busy tending to other customers. "What's a guy gotta do to get a drink around here?"

Remmy gave Gordon a hard look. "You alright? You look stressed out."

Gordon didn't answer. He took a twenty out of his front pocket and waved it over the bar. Mack noticed the movement but finished ringing up the customer he was assisting before bringing over a bottle of Budweiser.

"And a shot of Jack," Gordon said, promptly guzzling half of the beer.

"Better?" Remmy asked with raised eyebrows.

"Getting there," Gordon said as he watched Mack pour the shot on the bar in front of him. "Ask me again in a minute."

Gordon threw back the shot, letting it warm his gut for a couple of seconds before chasing it down with a swig of beer. Remmy shrugged nonchalantly, as if to say "whatever," and sipped his own beer.

"Next round's on me," Gordon said, feeling guilty for being short with his drinking buddy. "It's been a rough day, that's all."

"Your uncle?" Remmy inquired.

"Yeah, that and the neighbor took a spill on her steps this morning. I had to call the cops and paramedics."

"Oh, wow. Is she gonna be alright?"

Gordon shrugged. "I don't know. They took her away on a stretcher."

"Damn. Is she old?"

"Yeah, kind of," Gordon said, considering Shirley's age for the first time. "I'd guess late sixties or early seventies. And she's a big woman, so I'm sure all that extra weight didn't help matters."

Remmy shook his head. "Probably broke a hip or something. Old folks are always breaking hips."

Gordon considered this. "How long do you think it takes to recover from a broken hip? Any idea?"

"My mother broke her hip a couple of years before she died. She was in the hospital for about a week, if I remember right. But then she had to go to a rehab place for physical therapy and stuff. It was a whole thing."

"So she was out of commission for quite a while then?"

"Oh yeah," Remmy said, nodding. "She was never right again, either. I think that was the beginning of the end for her."

Gordon finished his beer and thumped it down on the bar, hoping to get Mack's attention. He felt a brief flash of remorse for what he had done, but that feeling was quickly overshadowed by the prospect that Shirley was unlikely to return home anytime soon.

Mack swapped the empty bottle for a fresh one, and Gordon pointed a finger at Remmy.

"And two shots of Jack."

29

A gray-striped tabby sauntered into the glare of the Cadillac's headlights as Gordon turned into the driveway, appearing unfazed by the approaching car. Gordon stepped on the gas, and the car lurched forward. He slammed on the brakes just in time to avoid hitting the shed at the end of the drive, but not before clipping the trash can and sending it tumbling into the backyard. He shifted the car into reverse, leaning over the steering wheel to look over the hood as he slowly backed up. He didn't see the arrogant cat's flattened body in the driveway as he had hoped, but he took some satisfaction in knowing he had scared the crap out of it. He slowly got out of the car, cursing his injured knee for making the task so difficult. He looked up at the darkened windows of Shirley's house and, after pushing aside a fleeting pang of guilt, felt a wave of relief.

"No nosey queshions today," Gordon slurred, wagging a finger at the house. He leaned on the trunk of the car as he circled around it, but slipped and fell the moment he stepped onto the slick surface of the snow-covered walkway. "Fuck you!" he bellowed, unsure of exactly where he was directing his anger. He continued to mutter a litany of senseless curses as he awkwardly got to his feet and ascended the front steps in a low crouch in case he slipped again. He swore at the lock for refusing to accept the key, but eventually got it right and opened the door.

"Ack! Fuck you!" he spat, this time directing the expletive at the clashing odors that assaulted him upon entering the house. The scent of bleach was present, but it was losing the battle against the rotting stench it was meant to eliminate.

"Fuck you, fuck you, fuck you!"

Gordon slammed the door behind him and half fell onto the bottom step of the living room stairs. He grabbed one of the two remaining bottles of bleach on the floor by the stairs, unscrewed the cap, and then used the house key to clear the seal on the mouth of the bottle. He used the same key to pry the cork out of the hole in the floor and inserted the funnel. He swayed as he poured the bleach, splashing much of the liquid onto his hand and the floor. The chemical odor stung his nostrils, but he didn't mind, as it made it impossible to smell anything else. After the last bit sloshed out, he tossed the empty bottle across the room, where it struck the wall and fell to the floor.

"Fuck you!" he hollered, then removed the funnel from the hole and threw it against the same wall. "Fuck you, too!"

Gordon used the banister to help him stand. He

glared at the hole in the floor and attempted to spit into it, missing by several inches. The hole blurred and became two before he looked away. He stood and made his way to the kitchen, cursing his bad knee with every step.

"Fuck you, fuck you, fuck you."

Gordon fetched a can of beer from the refrigerator and staggered backward into the side of the table as he slammed the door shut. Everything in the kitchen seemed to rattle, and Gordon looked to the cellar door, where the doorknob appeared to turn fractionally before returning to its original position. If he were sober, the sight would have frightened him, but in his current state, he felt only anger.

"You're dead, bitch!" he bellowed, kicking the door with his good leg. His injured leg couldn't support the shifted weight, and his knee buckled, causing him to fall to the floor, dropping the beer and pulling a chair down with him. Using the fallen chair to help him off the floor, Gordon stumbled to the end of the counter where the junk drawer was located. He threw open the drawer, took out the hammer, and spilled the box of nails onto the kitchen table. He leaned against the refrigerator, holding a nail in place with one hand and swinging the hammer with the other. He missed the nail, striking his thumb instead.

"Ah! Fuck you!"

He fetched another nail, the largest one on the table, and tried again. This time, the nail sank in with the first hit, but when he let go and struck it a second time with the hammer, it bent flat against the wood. The doorknob rattled with each blow, and Gordon envisioned Uncle Milton's hand turning it from the other side, desperate to escape the cellar before the door was permanently secured.

"Fuck you! You're dead!" Gordon wailed. "Go lie down!"

Gordon made several more attempts before successfully driving a nail into the doorframe at the proper angle. He repeated the process two more times, then tossed the hammer onto the table, where it slid off the other side and clunked onto the floor. The foul stench was suddenly very strong, and Gordon once again envisioned Uncle Milton's half-rotted corpse standing just on the other side of the door. He noticed that the towel on the floor was out of place, so he pushed it toward the door with his foot. It moved easily because it had dried out, so Gordon picked it up and threw it into the sink. He ran the faucet until the towel was thoroughly saturated, then threw it onto the floor in front of the door. He pushed it with the toe of his shoe until the gap was fully covered. He picked the beer can up off the floor, nearly toppling over as he did so. He shuffled into the living room and bumped the back of his head against the wall as he sat down on the sofa. When he opened the can, beer frothed out and spilled all over his lap, causing him to choke on the foam as he attempted to drink it. He whipped the can against the wall above the TV, spraying beer onto the ceiling.

"Fuck you!"

Picking up and fumbling with the cigarettes on the coffee table, he fished one out and pinched it between his teeth. The filter ignited when he tried to light the wrong end, and, realizing his mistake, grabbed it with his fingers. The cigarette stuck to his lip as he tried to pull it away, and he accidentally touched the burning filter, eliciting yet another, "Fuck you!"

Exhausted and tired of suffering so many defeats, Gordon fell over sideways on the sofa and closed his eyes. Despite the whirling sensation in his head, he soon slipped into unconsciousness.

When Gordon woke up, the lights he had left on before passing out stung his eyes. Spots floated at the edges of his vision. His mouth was dry, and his head felt as if it were full of water. He pushed himself into a sitting position on the sofa and, feeling the dampness on the front of his pants, briefly wondered if he'd pissed himself. The back of his hand hurt, and he noticed a pink rash on the skin that looked like a chemical burn. He tried to remember what he had been doing before falling asleep on the sofa, but he could barely form a thought. He saw the beer can on the floor by the TV but couldn't remember how or why it was there. A cigarette lay on the floor beside his foot, the end of the filter burnt black. He had no recollection of lighting the wrong end of a cigarette, but he knew what it meant. He had made that mistake before, but only when he was thoroughly wasted, which also explained why he couldn't remember anything.

He had blacked out again.

As he surveyed the room, he noticed an empty bottle of bleach on the floor to his left, with the funnel resting close by. His vision remained blurred at the edges, as if his eyes were still half asleep and not yet functioning properly. Something in that peripheral haze caught his attention, and he turned his head in that direction to bring it into focus. The thing lay on the floor near the foot of the stairs. It was thin and pale in color, a few inches in length.

"What the hell is that?" Gordon muttered, squinting at the unidentified object. He felt he should know what it was, but he couldn't quite put his finger on it.

That's what it is, he thought. *It's a finger.*

Gordon blinked his eyes, but his vision remained hazy. The finger began to move, standing up and pointing toward the ceiling. Then it bent and wriggled as if beckoning him.

Gordon gasped and tried to stand, but fell back onto the sofa when his knee gave out. He made a second attempt, this time successfully rising to his feet. He shambled across the room to stand beside the television with his back to the wall and the staircase. He could not see the finger from there, but it could not see him either.

Fingers don't have eyes, you idiot, the voice of reason said from the hazy depths of Gordon's mind.

It knows I'm here! Gordon argued. *Uncle Milton knows!*

Uncle Milton is dead, and that is not his finger. There is no finger.

Those words sounded reasonable. Much more so than the proposition of a dead man's finger poking through a hole in the floor.

But I saw it. Didn't I?

Look again.

Gordon sidestepped along the wall until the stairs dropped below his shoulder, allowing him to look between the spindles. He inched forward until the floor beyond the bottom step came into view. He saw the hole in the floor and the cork lying beside it on the bleach-stained floorboards.

"It's just the fucking cork," Gordon muttered, walking over and picking it up. "But how'd it get out of the hole? It was in there yesterday."

Wasn't it?

Gordon sat down on the steps and firmly inserted the cork into the hole. He looked over at the empty bottle and funnel on the floor and vaguely remembered pouring bleach into the hole after coming home from the bar. He shut his eyes and pinched the bridge of his nose, but the effort failed to yield any further memories. He just couldn't think straight.

"I need to lay off the booze for a couple of days," he said aloud, hoping the sound of his own words would carry more weight. "That's it. No drinking today. None."

Gordon stood and pushed the curtain of the front window aside. The streetlight was on, but the sky was beginning to brighten. He went into the kitchen to get some water and found plenty of it on the linoleum floor. The kitchen table was out of place with various-sized nails scattered on its surface. A toppled chair and a hammer lay on the wet floor, and Gordon followed the trail of puddles to the soaked towel at the foot of the cellar door. The door itself was still outlined with duct tape, but several more nails had been hammered into it along the edge above the doorknob, most of them bent at varying angles. Gordon shook his head and sighed.

"Maybe it'll make sense after I get some sleep," he mumbled, taking a glass from the cupboard and filling it up in the sink. He chugged the water, refilled the glass, and took it upstairs with him. He crawled into bed and pulled the covers over his head, which was already beginning to ache.

30

Gordon didn't turn on the light when he got up to use the bathroom, knowing it would only make it harder to fall back asleep again. He swayed over the toilet with his eyes closed, trying to direct the steam by sound alone but failing miserably. Returning to the bedroom, he saw what appeared to be a figure lying on the bed. Though barely visible in the shadows, the shape resembled a human form so closely that Gordon halted in his tracks. He knew it had to be an illusion created by the random arrangement of pillows and blankets, but now that his mind had formed the connection, he could see it as nothing else. He stood in the doorway, staring at the bed, trying to discern which parts were pillows and which were blankets and how they had so accurately replicated a human form. The blankets had somehow bunched up to create the perfect illusion of legs and two feet with toes pointing upward. The torso had to be made up of one or both pillows, and the head...

Gordon felt a tingling in his scalp. Even in the gloom, both pillows were clearly visible at the head of the bed due to their white pillowcases. The head of the figure—*the imaginary figure*, he reminded himself—appeared darker than the pillow on which it rested. And if the pillows were there, then what was creating the illusion of a torso? And what was the head?

The figure sat up.

Gordon stopped breathing. He was unable to move, completely paralyzed by fear. He could no longer rationalize what he was seeing, and his mind stopped searching for explanations. Unable to tear his eyes from the impossible sight, Gordon felt along the wall in search of the light switch. The bedside lamp came on, but it did not dispel the thing that ought to have been an illusion.

Uncle Milton sat on the bed, bent at the waist, with his back straight and legs stretched out in front of him. His arms hung limply at his sides, the backs of his hands resting on the mattress with fingers curled loosely over the palms. His head turned fractionally to face Gordon, but there were no eyes in the empty sockets. Two black holes outlined with dry, rust-colored blood bore into Gordon, despite lacking any apparent means to do so. Much of the flesh was missing from his face, most notably the nose and cheeks, where only thin strands of muscle and sinew remained. Age-yellowed teeth appeared longer than they should have in receded gums exposed by the absence of lips. The jaw dropped open, the fibrous tissue that had been holding it in place snapping like dry-rotted rubber bands. What remained of Uncle Milton's chin sagged against his throat, revealing the

U-shaped arrangement of his lower teeth, while the upper ones hung above like rectangular stalactites. Something stirred in the dark space at the back of the throat, but it was not the tongue, for that, too, was missing.

It was a rat.

The rodent's head and front paws emerged from the esophagus, its whiskers twitching curiously. It continued to crawl up and out of Uncle Milton's throat and then paused briefly before dropping down into his lap. The rat was coated in a dark, viscous substance that it began to groom off with its forepaws and tongue. Another rat appeared at the back of Uncle Milton's throat and dropped down beside the first. The head of a third appeared, but Gordon did not stick around to see that one fully emerge.

His legs started moving of their own accord, propelling him backward through the doorway. He turned and charged down the stairs, throwing his arm over the banister to catch himself when his bad knee gave out. He somehow reached the bottom, where he turned to see if he was being pursued. He reached for his coat on the chair beside the front door, keeping his eyes on the upstairs landing. A floorboard creaked, but Gordon did not wait to see what had caused the sound. He turned the deadbolt, pulled the door open, and fled into the cold night.

Gordon woke to the sound of a sharp tapping near

his left ear. He opened his eyes and, after a moment of disorientation, realized he was sitting behind the wheel of the Cadillac. The tapping came again. The sound startled him, and he pushed himself up in the seat. He looked around, but the windows were all fogged up, preventing him from seeing outside the car. The engine was running, and warm air blew steadily from the vents.

"Are you alright, Gordon?"

The muffled voice had come from outside the driver's side window. Gordon attempted to wipe the condensation from the glass with his sleeve, but quickly gave up and rolled down the window. Trey Booker stood just outside, looking concerned.

"Are you okay in there?" he asked, his eyes roaming the car's interior.

"Oh, yeah," Gordon croaked, then cleared his throat. "I was about to run out to the store, but I guess I dozed off while I was waiting for the engine to warm up."

"Oh, okay," said Trey, his eyes shifting to meet Gordon's. "I saw the fogged-up windows and wanted to make sure you hadn't left the car running unattended. You have to be careful in this neighborhood."

Gordon cleared his throat again. "Yeah, I appreciate that. Thanks."

"How's your uncle doing? My mom said you moved in to help out."

Gordon hoped his next excuse sounded as convincing as the first. "He hasn't been great lately," he said. "I was just about to get some more stuff for him at the store. Soup and tea, and stuff."

Trey looked over the top of the car toward the house, as if looking for some sign of Uncle Milton.

"How's your mom doing?" Gordon asked, hoping to change the subject.

Trey blew out a sigh. "She's not doing so great either. Turns out she cracked her pelvis and fractured her wrist when she fell. It's going to be a long recovery."

Gordon shook his head, hoping his inward smile didn't show.

"Thanks again for calling in the cavalry," Trey said, looking up the driveway to where the backyards met. "She might have frozen to death out there if you hadn't called for help."

"Ah, don't mention it," Gordon said. "What brings you by the house?"

Trey bent down and picked up a bag of dry cat food that he must have set down before tapping on the window. "She asked me to feed those cats she's so fond of." He shrugged. "She's been fretting over them in the hospital, so I told her I would take care of them."

Gordon nodded. "Do you need me to collect the mail or anything while she's away from home?"

"No, it's being delivered to my house for the time being. It will be a while before she's back in the house, but thanks for the offer. You can keep an eye on the place for us, though," he said, nodding toward the house. "Let us know if you see anybody snooping around."

"I will," Gordon said, shifting the car into reverse. "I'm gonna get over to the store now."

Trey stepped away from the car, shifting the cat food into the crook of his arm.

Before rolling up the window, Gordon said, "Tell Shirley I was asking about her."

31

Gordon lit his second cigarette after parking across the street from the establishment, which had a glowing red neon sign that read "PSYCHIC" in the front window. Another sign read, "SPIRITUAL ADVICE," while a third sign depicted a simple diagram of a hand with splayed fingers. He first noticed the place when he visited the pawn shop next door and had been thinking about it ever since Remmy told him how his niece had expelled the ghost from their house. He still had not returned to Uncle Milton's house since that horrific incident in the upstairs bedroom.

After the awkward conversation with Trey, Gordon bought his usual breakfast at the 7-11, which he ate in the car. He knew he would eventually have to return to the house, but he wanted to delay it for as long as possible. It would be at least another week before Uncle Milton's pension check landed in the account, which meant he would have to continue living there for at least that long. Stretching it out for another month would be even better. He still had nowhere near enough money to skip town and had yet to decide where he would go. Numerous decisions remained unaddressed. Will the authorities attempt to track him down once he's gone? Would they trace the Caddy, and if so, should he sell it? Should he change his identity, and if so, how on earth does one accomplish that?

Gordon's anxiety increased with every unanswered question, and every effort to silence them failed. He knew what would quiet those nagging thoughts, but he intended to delay his next drink for as long as possible. He did not want a repeat of the previous night. He did not want to black out again.

He had been driving around for the better part of an hour before passing the psychic sign. He circled the block, parked the car, and had been trying to muster the courage to go inside ever since. He had never visited a psychic before—had never even considered it. He wasn't sure what to do or how much it would cost.

The door across the street opened, and a middle-aged woman appeared in the doorway. She had long, dark hair and wore a simple, burgundy-colored dress. She looked directly at Gordon.

"Come on in," she said, just loud enough to be heard across the street. "I know you want to."

Gordon stared dumbly, unprepared for the unexpected greeting.

"Come on now," she said, beckoning with one hand. "I can help you. That is why you are here." The woman smiled, then turned and went back inside.

Gordon took a long drag from his cigarette. He wasn't sure if the woman had simply observed him staring at her establishment from across the street or if her psychic powers had alerted her of his presence. Either way, she had broken the ice and made up his mind for him. He got out of the car, took a final drag, and then flicked what was left of the cigarette into a nearby sewer grate. A bell chimed softly as he opened the door and entered a small waiting room with two cheap-looking chairs and a magazine rack. A velvet red curtain on the back wall shifted to the side, and the woman in the burgundy dress waved him in.

"Right this way," she said. "Don't be shy."

Gordon did as she asked and stepped through the curtain into a small, dimly lit space. Two chairs stood on opposite sides of a circular table in the center of the room. The tablecloth featured a symmetrical design, and similar-looking tapestries adorned the walls. A full bookshelf stood against one wall, but Gordon did not attempt to read any of the titles on the spines.

"You may sit," the woman said, gesturing to one of the chairs. "I am Lucinda."

Gordon licked his lips, which suddenly felt dry, and introduced himself.

"The first reading is fifty dollars," Lucinda said as Gordon pulled out the chair.

"Oh, I hope I have enough," Gordon said, reaching for

his wallet in his back pocket.

"If not, there is an ATM on the corner."

Gordon opened his wallet and removed all the cash inside. "I have forty-seven," he said.

"Close enough," Lucinda said, accepting the money. "Now, sit," she said, taking her own seat. "Something is troubling you, yes?" She gazed intently into Gordon's eyes as soon as he sat down. "Something... something very bad."

Gordon nodded.

"Something haunts you."

Gordon nodded again.

Lucinda gave him a knowing look and nodded. "I knew as soon as I saw you outside. I see it around you. It is with you now."

Gordon's skin tingled, and he shifted in his chair.

"What can you tell me about this spirit that haunts you?"

"He hates me," Gordon said, unsure why he had started with that. "I mean, I don't know. It... he scares me."

"So, you know this spirit then, yes? You knew him in life."

Gordon nodded and tried to swallow, but his throat was too dry.

"You are thirsty," Lucinda said. "I have water."

Without waiting for a reply, the psychic stood and walked out through a doorway hidden behind one of the tapestries. She returned a moment later and set a small, eight-ounce bottle of water on the table in front of Gordon.

"Tell me why he haunts you," Lucida said, returning to her seat.

Gordon unscrewed the cap and took a sip of water. "He wants me out of his," Gordon paused to rephrase his response. "I think he wants me out of the house."

"What does he do?"

"He… I see him, and he scares me. He's very scary."

"You see him?"

Gordon nodded.

"Where do you see him?"

Gordon reflected on what had happened in the bedroom, but also recalled the incidents involving the finger and the wheelchair. "In different parts of the house," he said. "Not all in one place."

"Is there a particular room in the house where the spirit's energy is strongest?" Lucinda asked. "A place where the entity dwells?"

"The cellar," Gordon said without thinking.

"Oh, underground," Lucinda said worryingly. "Only wicked spirits linger in those places. That is not good."

Gordon took another sip of water from the tiny bottle.

"You must take control of the situation," Lucinda said firmly. "You must banish this spirit. Send it off to the afterlife where it belongs."

"How do I do that?"

"I can do it," Lucinda said, folding her hands on the table. "I can come to the house and perform the banishing ritual, which involves walking through—"

"No!" Gordon blurted, interrupting the psychic mid-sentence. He could not allow anyone in the house.

Lucinda raised a questioning eyebrow. "You do not want me to come?"

"No, I just," Gordon stammered, trying to muster an excuse. "The house is a mess," he said. "I'm fixing it up, doing some construction and stuff."

"Ah," Lucinda said, unlacing her fingers and spreading her hands apart. "That explains a lot. Changes to an old house can disturb sleeping spirits. I have seen it before. Many times." She turned in her chair and opened a chest on the floor behind her, which Gordon had not noticed before. "You can perform the ritual yourself," she said over her shoulder. "I will show you how." She rummaged through the chest for a full minute before straightening up and placing several items on the table.

"What's all that stuff?" Gordon asked.

Lucinda tapped a piece of clear crystal with her index finger. "This crystal will protect you," she said.

"Keep it with you at all times." She picked up a small, circular pendant that appeared to be made of pewter. There were tiny symbols or runes engraved on it, and it had a loop at the top to hold the thin cord, allowing it to be worn as a necklace. "This amulet will also keep you safe. Wear it around your neck at all times." She held it out over the table by the cord, which Gordon took to mean he should put it on, so he did. "And this," she said, picking up what looked like a bunch of dried leaves tied into a bundle with string. "This is sage for you to burn inside the house. The smoke will cleanse the space of negative energy. You must walk all through the house while reciting the words of banishment. And you must believe. You must have faith in the words you speak."

"Words?" Gordon asked. "What words?"

"Don't worry, I will write them down for you."

Gordon drew a long breath and released it. "Is that it? Is that all I have to do? Then he—the spirit—will stop bothering me?"

"It should work," Lucinda said, tilting her head, though her expression did not convey complete confidence. "It usually does. If not, come back, and we will try something else."

"Okay," Gordon said, standing and wincing as he put weight on his bad knee.

Lucinda waved a hand over the items on the table. "The sage, the crystal, and the medallion are sixty dollars."

Gordon looked at her, surprised by the unexpected charge.

"It's usually eighty," she said, "but I am giving you a package deal."

Gordon sighed and walked to the ATM on the corner. When he returned with the money, Lucinda gave him a page torn from a small notepad containing the words he was meant to recite during the cleansing ritual. She explained the ritual to him in simple terms, and Gordon thanked her as he walked out the door with his spirit-banishing arsenal. He tucked the crystal into his pants pocket and set the sage on the passenger seat after getting into the car. He felt the amulet hanging around his neck and couldn't decide whether its presence comforted or unsettled him. Lucinda told him that he had to believe in the charms and the spell—or whatever it was—for it to work, but he wasn't sure if he wanted to believe any of it.

32

Cormack's was packed, with every bar stool occupied. Gordon spotted Remmy and shouldered up beside him. He waved a twenty in the air, catching Mack's eye as he moved from one end of the bar to the other.

"Why's it so busy?" Gordon asked Remmy over the din.

"It's the last Saturday before Christmas," Remmy said, leaning back on his stool to look around the bar. "Holiday cheer and all that, I guess."

Mack set a bottle of Budweiser in front of Gordon, but before he could move on to the next customer, Gordon held up two fingers. Mack knew exactly what that meant and quickly poured two shots of Jack Daniel's, working faster than usual.

"Here's to Christmas being over," Gordon said, spilling some whiskey as he shakily lifted the glass and downed the shot.

"Bah humbug!" Remmy said before downing his own shot.

"I hate Christmas," Gordon said, glaring down the length of the bar. He didn't appreciate all these strangers in the place he considered his refuge.

"Yeah, I'll be glad when it's over," Remmy agreed.

Gordon took a long swig of beer. "Next round's on you."

"Do you have family coming in?" Remmy asked. "Or will it just be you and your uncle this year?"

The question reminded Gordon why he had come to the bar, and something unpleasant fluttered in his stomach. He had driven to the house after his visit with the psychic, but he was so overwhelmed by a sense of dread that he didn't even pull into the driveway. He went to the liquor store and, despite intending to refrain from drinking for a while, bought a twelve-pack of beer and a pint of whiskey. The image of Uncle Milton's rotting corpse sitting up in his bed replayed in his mind every moment he wasn't distracted by something else, and he knew he couldn't delay the inevitable any longer. He was tempted to go back to the house and drink the liquid courage in the driveway before going inside, but he worried that Trey might show up to feed those detestable cats and interrupt him. That left Cormack's as the only logical option, and once his mind was made up, the car practically drove itself to the bar.

"My sister won't be coming this year," Gordon said. "Her husband got cancer."

"Oh, shit. I'm sorry to hear that."

Gordon shrugged. "Life sucks, and then you die."

Remmy nodded in agreement, then asked, "Has there been any more activity at the house?"

"Activity?"

"Yeah, you know. With that ghost of yours."

Gordon winced inwardly. He assumed Remmy was trying to direct their conversation to a lighter topic, unaware that he was doing the exact opposite. His initial instinct was to say no and avoid the matter entirely, but then he reconsidered. Maybe his friend could help. After all, he was the one who had some knowledge of a haunting, albeit second-hand. "There was something, actually," he said. "I saw something in the upstairs bedroom last night."

"Oh yeah?" Remmy said, intrigued. "What happened?"

Gordon knew he couldn't tell Remmy that he had seen Uncle Milton since everyone was supposed to think he was still alive, so he tried to be as vague as possible. "I woke up in the middle of the night to take a leak, and when I went back to my room, I saw a person lying in my bed."

"Oh shit!" Remmy exclaimed. "That must've scared the livin' crap out of you!"

"Yeah, it did. I hightailed it right outta there. I didn't go back to bed, and I haven't been back to the house since."

"Damn. Did you see it clearly? What did it look like?"

Gordon closed his eyes, and the image of Uncle

Milton's animated corpse flashed behind his eyelids. He suddenly wished he hadn't brought it up. "Just some guy, sitting up in the bed," he said, opening his eyes to banish the image.

"Damn! And you're sure it wasn't a dream?"

"Positive. I wasn't asleep."

"Could it have been a trick of the light or something?"

"I turned the light on, and he was still there."

"Holy shit!" Remmy said, turning and staring wide-eyed at Gordon. "Did you tell your uncle?"

Gordon groaned, but not loud enough to be heard in the noisy bar. He closed his eyes, then immediately reopened them. "No," he said, picking up his beer and draining it. "How about that round? It's your turn to buy."

"Yeah, okay," Remmy said, finishing his own beer and placing it at the far edge of the bar. "So what are you gonna do?"

"I went to a psychic lady," Gordon said, looking down the bar where Mack was busy mixing a drink. "I'm gonna try doing what your niece did."

"Oh, that's good. Is she gonna come to the house?"

"No, she wrote down some words for me to say and gave me some stuff to burn."

"Sage?"

"Yeah," Gordon said, slightly surprised by Remmy's

accurate assumption.

"That's good," Remmy said, nodding. "That's what the spiritualist woman used at my sister's place. It seems to have worked for them."

"Sorry for butting in, but I couldn't help overhearing."

Gordon turned to the man on the stool directly to his left. He wore a stylish sweater, and a martini glass sat on the bar in front of him.

"You said you saw something you couldn't explain?" the man said, a quizzical expression on his clean-shaven face.

"He said he saw a ghost," Remmy cut in before Gordon could respond. "No explanation required."

The man raised a placating hand. "I don't mean to offend. I just thought I'd offer a possible explanation."

"Like I said," Remmy said, making his irritation known. "No explanation required."

"It's all right," Gordon said, elbowing his friend. He was curious to hear what the stranger had to say. "How would you explain what I saw?"

"Well," the man said, "it is not unusual to see things, to hallucinate when the mind is not operating at full capacity."

"Yeah?" Remmy interjected, "What's that supposed to mean?"

Gordon elbowed Remmy again. "Let him talk."

"The brain is more prone to hallucinations when not fully awake or impaired."

"But I turned the light on," Gordon argued. "And I saw him clear as day."

"Hallucinations can be very convincing."

"What makes you an expert?" Remmy asked, unable to remain quiet.

"I'm a psychiatrist," the man said, offering his hand to Gordon. "Francis Price."

Gordon awkwardly accepted the handshake, but Remmy turned away and sipped his beer when the doctor extended his hand toward him.

"I think I would know if I was hallucinating," Gordon said. "What I saw wasn't fuzzy or blurry or anything."

"Had you been drinking before going to bed?"

Gordon didn't answer immediately, and he could tell the doctor took that as a yes.

"Alcohol consumption impairs REM sleep and the ability to dream, which is a necessary function of the brain. If a person drinks excessively on a regular basis and does not dream enough while sleeping, the brain may attempt to do so while the individual is awake— or partially awake—causing hallucinations."

"Why don't you mind your own fuckin' business?" Remmy interjected, leaning over the bar in front of Gordon. "Nobody asked you anyway."

"Is there a problem here?" Mack said, stopping

midstride with a drink in each hand.

Gordon shook his head, but Remmy continued to leer at the doctor.

"No problem," Dr. Price said, taking one final sip of his drink before standing up. "I was just leaving. You can take my seat. Happy Holidays, gentlemen."

All three men watched the doctor leave the bar, and Mack said, "I don't know what you did, but I don't appreciate you guys chasing customers out of my bar."

"Fuck him," Remmy said, unfazed by Mack's scolding. "The dick doesn't know how to mind his own business." He gathered the empty bottles and shot glasses and pushed them to the edge of the bar like a poker player betting all-in with his chips. "Another round for me and Gordy, Mack. On me."

Gordon patted Remmy on the back and sat down on the vacated stool. He appreciated his friend for having his back, but he had wanted to hear the doctor out. He still wasn't sure what to believe about what had happened at the house. Admitting that he had been hallucinating was not an easy thing to do, but it was better than the alternative. *Wasn't it?*

"Don't let that prick get to you, Gordy," Remmy said. "Those shrinks think they know it all. They think everything can be explained with science and book talk. You know what you saw. People see ghosts all the time."

"Yeah, I guess," Gordon said, glancing toward the

door. "But it did kinda make sense, the way he put it."

"You were wide awake with the lights on, Gordy. He was just fishing for explanations. And it ain't the only thing that happened in that house, right?" Remmy said, as if stating the obvious. "That guy doesn't know the whole story."

Mack placed two beers on the bar and refilled the shot glasses with Jack Daniel's.

"Burn that sage and whatever else that spiritualist told you to do, and you'll be good to go," Remmy said, picking up one of the shots. "Here's to being rid of that ghost."

Gordon picked up the other shot. "I'll drink to that."

Someone at the other end of the bar spilled a drink, and the people around him erupted in a chorus of cheers and jeers.

"Cut him off, Mack!" Remmy shouted as Mack hurried toward the scene of the accident with a rag in one hand.

Gordon chuckled and washed the shot down with a long swig of Budweiser. The shot warmed his gut, and a mist began to rise in his mind, shrouding his worries and dulling his thoughts.

33

The Cadillac bucked over the curb as Gordon made the turn onto Uncle Milton's street. As he pulled into the driveway, he noticed that the light was still on in the upstairs bedroom. He couldn't shake the thought that his uncle's corpse might still be sitting upright in the bed, blood-soaked rats grooming themselves in his lap.

"Fuck you!" Gordon said, verbally cursing the image that appeared in his mind. He grabbed the bundle of sage from the passenger seat and tucked it into his coat pocket. He popped the trunk and walked around to the back of the car. As he reached for the beer and whiskey he'd bought earlier in the day, Gordon noticed the tire iron tucked in one corner. He thought he could use it when the time came to pry open the cellar door, so he took it from the trunk along with the booze. He carried everything up the walk to the house, favoring his bad leg as he ascended the front steps. His injured knee remained swollen and showed no signs of improvement. He set the liquor and the tire iron down on the bench by the front door, glancing through the front window as he did so. The light was on in the kitchen at the back of the house, but it only made the living room appear gloomier than usual. He felt Lucinda's crystal in his pocket as he dug out his keys, which prompted him to reach for the amulet around his neck. He felt the circular shape through his shirt, and although the protective items offered him some comfort, they also reminded him of why they were necessary. Gordon's anxiety had gradually increased since leaving the bar, and it took a significant force of will to insert the key into the lock and open the door.

The stench from inside was strong enough to make him take a step backward.

"Fuck!"

Gordon's first thought was to get back in the car and return to Cormack's, but he knew that would only delay the inevitable. He eyed the liquor on the bench and promised himself that he would reward himself with a beer and a shot once he was inside. He drew a long breath and held it, leaving the front door open as he entered the house. He marched directly toward the kitchen, ignoring the pain in his leg. He opened the window over the sink and immediately felt the draft move through the house, front to back. He released the air in his lungs, triggering a coughing fit that, oddly enough, made him crave a cigarette. Returning to the front porch, he grabbed the beer and whiskey from the bench and brought them inside. He opened the front window to keep the cross draft flowing before closing the front door. The temperature inside dropped quickly, but the air quality dramatically improved.

How long is that smell going to last?

The question prompted Gordon to look at the corked hole in the floor at the foot of the stairs and the last remaining bottle of bleach sitting nearby. His approach to the problem was clearly ineffective, but he couldn't think of another way to eliminate the smell without going into the cellar. The thought of seeing Uncle Milton's corpse was bad enough, but the idea of doing anything at all with the body was even more repulsive.

You're going to have to open the door anyway, he reminded himself. *To banish his spirit.*

Lucinda told him that he would have to address the negative energy where it was strongest. She told him first to cleanse every room in the house with smoke from the sage while reciting the words she had written down for him. He was then to complete the ritual in the place where the spirit was strongest: at the source. He knew the source had to be Uncle Milton's body, which meant that the cellar was the place where the negative energy was strongest. She told him to make a clear path for the spirit to leave the house by opening a door or window. He had already opened the window over the kitchen sink, which was situated directly across from the cellar door, so at least that much was already done.

But you will have to open the cellar door.

Gordon grabbed the whiskey bottle from the chair by the front door and unscrewed the cap. He did it without thinking, his body going through the motions as a natural response to the fear and anxiety brought on by the prospect of what lay ahead. He took a swig from the bottle, immediately grateful for the distraction granted by the sting of alcohol on his tongue and the back of his throat. He set the whiskey on the coffee table and tore open the twelve-pack. He sat down on the sofa and switched on the TV, eager to fill the house with the sound of normalcy. He scrolled through the channels until settling on the old Christmas classic, *It's a Wonderful Life*. He opened the beer and lit a cigarette. He removed the sage from his coat pocket and held it under his nose. It had the scent of mint and pine, and Gordon hoped burning it would banish the stink along with Uncle Milton's spirit. He removed the paper Lucina had given him from his pocket and slowly read the words she had written down for him.

Leave this space now, I command you to depart.

I cleanse this area with the power of sage, be gone.

By the power of the sacred herb, I
banish you from this place.

Gordon envisioned himself reciting those words as he walked around the house with the burning sage and shook his head. Reading alone was bad enough, but reading aloud was even worse. *What if I mess it up?*

Will that make things worse?

Once again, the whiskey bottle was in Gordon's hand, but he decided to mix himself a Jack and Coke instead of drinking straight from the bottle. He prepared the drink in the kitchen, and despite his efforts, he found it impossible to ignore the cellar door, outlined with duct tape and riddled with bent nails. He brought the drink and the bottle back into the living room and chugged the rest of the beer, not wanting it to go to waste. A cold draft swept through the room, prompting Gordon to lower the front window, leaving a gap of a few inches open at the bottom. On the TV, George Bailey and the guy who claimed to be an angel were ordering drinks at the local bar. The angel requested mulled wine, heavy on the cinnamon and light on the cloves.

One of the radiators made a popping noise, followed by a series of ticks and taps. The sounds spread upward through the house as hot water moved through the pipes. Gordon tracked the sound with his eyes, up the stairs and toward the ceiling. He was reminded that he had not yet checked the upstairs bedroom—not yet checked to see if Uncle Milton still sat on the bed. Now that he had thought about it, he could think of nothing else. He gulped down half of his drink and lit another cigarette. He turned up the volume on the TV. He knew he was procrastinating and that he could not delay the inevitable for much longer.

One more drink, and I'll be good to go.

34

Gordon slowly climbed the stairs. He decided to start the banishing ritual upstairs and work his way down through the house, but had lit the sage in the living room, wanting every protection in place when he entered the upstairs bedroom. He had the talisman still around his neck and the crystal in his pocket. He held the bundle of smoldering herbs in one hand, the paper with Lucinda's handwritten words in the other. His injured knee forced him to take the stairs one at a time, but the slow ascent also allowed the smoke to reach the second floor ahead of him, which was precisely what he wanted. He waved the sage in the air to coax the embers, and Gordon was impressed by the volume of smoke it produced. He peered into the bedroom before reaching the landing and was relieved to find no corpse in the bed. He entered the room, holding the burning sage out in front of him. Smoke billowed up to the ceiling before spreading outward in all directions. Gordon lifted the paper and adjusted its distance from his eyes until the words came into focus.

"Leave this place now," he began, enunciating each

word stiffly, much like a child reading aloud in class. "I command you to depart. As the smoke rises, take your negative energy with it. By the power of the sacred herb," Gordon paused, then repeated the last word, omitting the 'H' sound. He tested the word both ways several times before deciding to pronounce it as it was written, with the 'H', before following up with the final line on the page: "I banish you from this place."

Looking up from the paper, Gordon listened for any unusual sounds in the house. He heard the television downstairs and wondered if he should have turned it off before starting the ritual. He moved next into Uncle Milton's old bedroom and waved the sage around before reciting the words for the second time. The burning sage felt like a weapon of sorts in his hand, providing him with a sense of security. He repeated the process in the upstairs bathroom and then slowly started down the stairs. He stopped before reaching the bottom, as the house was suddenly filled with a series of clanking sounds. He knew that the pipes and radiators were responsible for the racket, but it was much louder than usual this time. It seemed to Gordon that the house was responding to the banishing ritual, which he found both reassuring and frightening at the same time. Standing still allowed the smoke to envelop him, and he coughed as he broke free from the cloud and descended the last few steps. It was noticeably cooler downstairs, and the smoke from the sage flowed with the outside air as it slowly moved through the house. He recited the spell in the living room, and the radiator nearest him made a strange, groaning sound. He could feel the heat radiating from it and tentatively touched one of the metal conduction fins with the hand holding the paper.

"Fuck, that's hot!" he hissed, bringing the singed finger to his lips and blowing on it.

Gordon passed through the kitchen and into Uncle Milton's bedroom. He delivered the recitation once again, the words flowing more easily after so many repetitions. He repeated the process in the bathroom and kitchen, then stood before the cellar door.

A deafening bang, loud enough to rattle the entire house, erupted from under the floor. Gordon flinched so violently that the sage flew from his hand. He immediately knelt to pick it up, but his knee refused to bend, and he fell forward onto his hands, dropping the paper in the process. He snatched up the sage and rolled onto his backside, groaning and cursing all the while. He blew on the sage and waved it in the air, but most of the glowing embers had broken off when it struck the floor. With the aid of a kitchen chair, Gordon rose to his feet and hobbled over to the stove. He turned on one of the gas burners and held the sage in the flame until the bundle caught fire. He allowed it to burn for a long moment before blowing it out, and smoke once again billowed from the smudge stick.

As he turned around, Gordon noticed the uncapped bottle of bourbon on the kitchen table. He picked it up and took several large gulps. The whiskey burned his throat and nose, nearly making him vomit as his stomach struggled to handle so much alcohol at once. Gordon slammed the bottle onto the table and leaned back against the counter to relieve the pressure on his throbbing knee. He swooned as alcohol-rich blood reached his head, but it also provided him with the boost of courage he so desperately needed.

"Alright, motherfugger," Gordon slurred at the cellar door. "Time for you to get the fuck outta here!"

Gordon half fell toward the door and grabbed hold of the doorknob to catch himself. It turned in his hand, and he jerked away from the door, unsure whether he had turned the knob or if someone on the other side had done it.

Another loud bang from the cellar shook the floor.

"Fuck you motherfucker!" Gordon shouted at the top of his lungs. Fueled by alcohol-induced courage and anger, Gordon grasped the doorknob with his free hand and twisted it with more force than necessary. He tugged on the knob, but the door didn't budge. He wavered there, with his hand on the doorknob to steady himself. The nails that had been hammered in at eye level came into focus, prompting Gordon to mutter several curses at himself for forgetting about them. He staggered over to the junk drawer and took out the hammer. He balanced the smoldering sage on the edge of the counter next to the refrigerator and began removing the nails from the door. The task was not easy under normal circumstances, and Gordon's increasingly inebriated state only made it more difficult. He managed to remove two of the bent ones but failed repeatedly when he tried to get the claw end of the hammer around the heads of the others.

"Fuck you! Fuck you! Fuck you!"

Gordon repeatedly struck the door with the hammer, pounding it again and again. He swung it toward the doorknob, but it deflected off the metal, causing the hammer to slam into his bad knee. Gordon cried out in blinding agony. The pain was so intense that he felt he might pass out, so he bent over the counter until it gradually lessened to a more tolerable level. When he could once again form a thought amid the pain and anger consuming him, he remembered the tire iron he had taken from the car.

"Fuckin' idiot!"

Gordon limped to the front door, muttering curses with each step. He found the tire iron where he'd left it on the porch and brought it inside, slamming the door behind him. He limped back to the kitchen like a man who'd been shot in the leg. Balancing awkwardly on one leg in front of the cellar door, he inserted the flat end of the tire iron into the gap between the door and the frame above the doorknob. He leaned his weight into it, and the nails squealed and groaned as the door slowly pulled free of the frame. Wood splintered around the jam, and the door swung open.

Gordon retched as the stench hit him, dropping the

tire iron on the floor. His senses reeled against the combined odor of bleach and rotting flesh. He held his breath as he grabbed the smoking sage from the counter and waved it in front of the doorway. He realized he no longer had the banishing spell and quickly glanced around the kitchen to find it. He did not see the paper anywhere, but a sudden movement drew his attention to the lower part of the doorway. Something shot up and out of the cellar, and Gordon yelped as a rat ran over his foot. It was immediately followed by a second and then a third. The rodents were in a state of panic, and one of them began to scramble up Gordon's pant leg. Before he could swat it away, something else leaped onto Gordon from the other direction.

Snowball.

The white cat's claws pierced the fabric of his jeans and then his shirt as it chased the rodent up his body. Gordon spun in place, shouting nonsense as he flailed at the animals frantically crawling over him. From the corner of his eye, he saw more cats entering through the open window over the sink and dropping to the floor, where rats continued to pour out of the cellar and scatter in all directions. The rat that was climbing on him reached his shoulder and bit into his hand when he tried to brush it off. Snowball hissed and writhed wildly as it tried to free its claws, which were caught on the fabric of Gordon's shirt and the skin beneath. The rat finally let go when Gordon flung his hand away from his body, but he lost his balance in the process. He reached behind him to grab hold of something to keep himself from falling, but he found only empty air.

Gordon fell backward through the open doorway, landing headfirst on a wooden stair halfway down before tumbling to the bottom, where Uncle Milton waited.

35

Gordon and Manny sat on a bench in a secluded corner of the park down the street from Brenda Gilmartin's house. The two seventeen-year-olds shared a six-pack of Michelob and a half-pint of blackberry brandy that Manny's older brother had bought for them in exchange for a car wash and enough cash to buy something for himself. The date was October 29, 1983.

"Everyone is going," Manny said. "Even Simeon Kulak."

"Really?" Gordon said, pausing with the brandy halfway to his lips. "Simpleton is going?"

"Yep," Manny affirmed. "It was probably a pity-invitation, but whatever."

Gordon frowned and took a generous swig of the sweet liqueur. He had not been invited to Brenda's Halloween party. Manny had said that Brenda suggested he should "come by," but it seemed to Gordon that she only said that because they were in the same biology class and had already invited Manny's lab partner, David Higgins.

"That's why it won't be a big deal if you show up," Manny said. "Like I said, just about every senior is going anyway."

Gordon nodded, but he still wished he had been invited. He tried to convince himself that he'd been overlooked because he wasn't in any of Brenda's classes, but he couldn't help but feel dejected. Brenda was super-popular and way out of his league. She hung out with cheerleaders and jocks, and Gordon only ever hung out with Manny. He couldn't even meet her eyes when they passed each other in the halls, so why would she invite him?

"It'll be fine," Manny said, likely noticing Gordon's body language. "You'll walk in with me, and nobody will say anything."

Gordon nodded, but he remained unconvinced. Sounds of people arriving at Brenda's could be heard from down the street, causing Gordon's anxiety to ramp up. He took another swig of brandy.

"Easy there, Flash," Manny said, using the nickname inspired by the Flash Gordon movie that was released a few years earlier. "You're gonna get wasted."

"It's just brandy," Gordon said with a shrug.

"It'll still mess you up." The sound of raised voices and car doors slamming drifted down the block, and Manny turned to look in that direction. "We should probably head over there."

"You didn't even drink your last beer yet," Gordon

said, nodding to the paper bag on the ground beside the bench.

"I'm good," Manny said. "I don't want to show up wasted. I'll drink it later."

"It's gonna get warm," Gordon argued.

"It's cool enough out here, and it's just gonna get colder. It'll be fine." He moved the bag behind the bench, where it was less visible. "Let's go."

"After a cigarette," Gordon said, wishing to stall as long as possible. He tapped a Marlboro out of the pack and lit up before Manny could voice an argument. He picked up his nearly empty beer bottle from the ground and squinted at the scant contents through the amber-tinted glass. "And I still have some beer left."

Manny lit his own cigarette.

"Where's your costume?" Gordon asked. "You said to bring something."

"I heard people are dressing up, but I doubt everyone will." Manny reached into his coat pocket, pulled out a pair of Groucho Marx novelty glasses with an attached plastic nose and mustache, and put them on.

Gordon flapped his lips. "That's so lame," he said, reaching into his own coat and removing a cheap rubber mask. He slipped it over his head, where it hung loosely over his face.

"Like that's any better," Manny said, rolling his eyes.

Gordon removed the mask. "I'm just gonna wear it when we walk in, then I'll take it off. If anyone asks where my costume is, I'll show 'em."

"What is it even supposed to be?" Manny asked, taking the mask from Gordon and examining it.

"I don't really know," Gordon admitted. "I ordered it from a comic book when I was a kid. I think it's supposed to be a ghoul or something."

"It doesn't look like anything to me," Manny said, tossing the mask back to Gordon. "Just a droopy face with eye slits."

"Yeah, well, at least it's something." Gordon stuffed the rubber mask back into his coat pocket.

"And you think mine is lame?" Manny blew out a lungful of smoke. "You should have worn red tights and gone as Flash Gordon."

"Fuck you," Gordon said before pouring the last, flat sip of beer onto his tongue.

Manny stood and stamped out his cigarette. "Let's go."

The guys walked down the street to find several cars, including Simeon Kulak's shiny red Nova, parked in front of Brenda's house.

"I see Simpleton is already here," Gordon said.

Yeah," said Manny. "That sure is one badass ride."

Gordon didn't respond, but he had to admit he was jealous. Simeon Kulak's Nova had turned heads when he pulled into the lot on the first day of school, and people still talked about it. Some of the other kids got their driver's licenses over the summer and showed up with cars of their own for senior year, but none were more impressive than Simeon's 1976 Nova. He claimed to have paid for the car with his own money and a small loan from his parents. Simpleton, as he had been commonly known since grammar school, had gone from zero to hero in an instant. Most people had even stopped referring to him by his lifelong nickname. Gordon had never done well in school, and his grades reflected that, but at least he'd always been smarter than Simeon "Simpleton" Kulak. Now, the "slow kid" had become popular enough to receive an invitation to Brenda Gilmartin's Halloween party, while Gordon was showing up as a party crasher, without a car.

Music and raised voices could be heard coming from inside the house. Gordon felt grateful for the alcohol buzz, which eased his anxiety to some degree. Manny put on his Groucho Marx glasses and rang the doorbell. Gordon took out his mask, but he didn't put it on. He suddenly felt foolish for bringing it and wished he had given more thought to his costume. The door opened, and Brenda, dressed as an Indian squaw, appeared in the doorway.

"Hi Manny," Brenda said, then looked at Gordon. "I didn't know you were bringing anyone."

"I told Gordy he could tag along," Manny said. "I hope you don't mind."

Gordon felt his cheeks burning. He wished his friend hadn't phrased it that way. And Brenda Gilmartin hadn't even mentioned his name.

"Come on in," she said, stepping away from the door. "Everyone's in the garage."

They followed the sound of ZZ Top's *Eliminator* album through the kitchen and into the garage, which was decorated with black and orange streamers and paper cutouts of witches and skeletons. There were at least thirty kids in the spacious two-car garage, all divided into small groups. All the girls wore costumes, but less than half of the guys were dressed up. Mark Mason and several of his teammates were dressed in their football uniforms, which struck Gordon as a pretty good compromise, despite his dislike of that crew. David Higgins wore a Viking helmet and stood talking to Reggie Thomas, who was dressed as a vampire. Simeon Kulak stood alone by the garage door, dressed in an ill-fitting Boy Scout uniform he had long since outgrown. Gordon followed Manny to a long table adorned with a variety of cookies, cupcakes, an assortment of soda cans, and a large punchbowl.

"I wonder if the punch is spiked," Gordon said, elbowing his friend.

"I highly doubt it," Manny said, grabbing a pumpkin-shaped cookie and taking a bite.

"There's still some brandy left," Gordon said, patting his coat where the bottle rested in an inside pocket.

"Don't even think about it," Manny said under his

breath. "Not with this crew. You'll get us thrown out."

"We could mix our own," Gordon said, wiggling his eyebrows.

Cathy Wheeler, who was one of two girls dressed as a cat, tapped Manny on the shoulder, and the two started talking, leaving Gordon to stare at his friend's back. He helped himself to a cup of punch and scanned the room for someone to talk to. He was terribly awkward around girls, so he walked over to David and Reggie, who were laughing about something.

"What's so funny?" Gordon asked.

David nodded at Beverly Tuffin, who was wearing a cheerleader outfit and swaying gently to the music while talking with one of the football players.

"Reggie here said he'd like to sample Beverly Tuffin's muffin," and all three erupted into laughter.

After taking a sip of punch, Gordon said, "This could use a bit of help." He then handed the cup to David, who accepted it with a curious look. Gordon offered a conspiratorial grin and reached inside his coat. He unscrewed the cap with one hand and took the bottle of brandy out of his pocket, using one side of his coat to hide his actions. He poured a generous splash of brandy into the cup in David's hand and put the bottle back in his pocket.

"Oh, shit," Reggie said as he and David looked around nervously.

"Get some punch if you want some," Gordon said,

taking the cup from David, who appeared glad to be rid of it.

The guys exchanged glances, and David said, "Maybe in a little while. I'm not thirsty right now."

"Yeah, maybe later," Reggie echoed.

"Don't wait too long," Gordon said. "It ain't gonna last all night."

"Hey, look," David said, elbowing Reggie and nodding toward the door. "Marty's here."

The two of them hurried over to greet Marty Glick, who appeared surprised by the unexpected attention. Gordon could tell they were looking for an excuse to break away, and he suddenly felt alone in the crowded room. He had hoped his covert offer would win the guys over, but it had clearly made them uncomfortable. Gordon drained his cup, and the combination of sweet liqueur and sugary punch was almost too much to bear. He went over to the table, where he exchanged his empty cup for a ginger ale. He swayed back on his heels as he popped the tab on the can, surprised by how quickly the brandy was affecting him. The three beers he had downed in the park had primed his blood alcohol level, and every sip of brandy was pushing him closer to full-blown intoxication. Simeon approached the table with his head down, looking nervous and uncomfortable around so many people. Gordon felt relieved to see someone who seemed even more out of place than he did, which boosted his self-confidence. He had never had a genuine conversation with Simeon. Previous interactions had always involved one-sided teasing from Gordon. With nothing better to do, he decided some light-hearted ribbing would do them both some good.

"Simpleton in da house!" Gordon said, much louder than he'd intended.

Simeon glanced at Gordon before quickly lowering his gaze to his feet. Heads turned to look at Gordon. Alison Kowalski, dressed like Madonna but not quite pulling it off, seemed to appear out of nowhere, positioning herself between Gordon and Simeon.

"Why do you have to be such an ass, Flash?" she said, pointing an accusatory finger at his face.

Gordon felt his face burning. Everyone was looking at him. He glanced around the garage, searching for Manny, but he was nowhere to be found; likely off somewhere making out with Cathy Wheeler. Brenda shot Gordon an angry glare before pulling Simeon aside to talk to him. Mark Mason appeared beside Alison, accompanied by two other football players.

"I got this, Alison," he said, putting a hand on Gordon's shoulder and leaning in toward his ear. "I think it's time you leave, Flash," he said. "You had your fun, now get going before things turn ugly."

"I was just messing around," Gordon said, forcing an innocent smile. "Sim knows I was. We're good."

"You're not good," Mark said, crowding even more

into Gordon's personal space. "You can do this the easy way or the hard way. What's it gonna be?"

"Aright, aright," Gordon said with a noticeable slur.

"He's drunk!" Alison-Madonna said, poking her head around the side of Mark's oversized shoulder pads.

Gordon held up his hands in mock surrender, turned, and headed for the door. He hurried through the kitchen and to the front door, eager to get out of the house. He opened the door and saw Brenda and Alison walking toward him through the living room as he turned to close it behind him. He heard the deadbolt set in the lock as he stepped off the porch. He started running when he reached the street and was soon back at the bench at the back of the park.

By the time he was halfway through Manny's leftover beer, Gordon had come up with a plan to save face. He would play a lighthearted prank on Simpleton, and they would both share a laugh together. He would give Simeon a big high-five in front of everyone, showing that Gordon hadn't meant any harm at the party. He might even persuade Simpleton to give him a ride home, since he lived on Gordon's side of town anyway. He would flatter Simeon with compliments about his car and tell him he had always wanted to go for a ride in it. Everyone would see the two of them leaving together, and everyone would know that Gordon wasn't the bully he'd appeared to be at the party.

Gordon finished the beer and the rest of the brandy,

then walked back toward Brenda's house, staying in the shadows to avoid being seen by anyone who might come outside. After confirming the coast was clear, he crossed the street and tried the door of Simeon's Nova. Had the door been locked, he would have had to revise his plan, but luck was on his side, and he got into the backseat, quietly closing the door behind him. He put on his rubber mask and lay down on the floor, where he would wait for Simeon and the others. He saw the prank unfolding in his mind's eye, saw everyone laughing after Gordon gave Simpleton a little scare, and then the high-five. He closed his eyes, and although he tried to stay awake, he gradually drifted off to sleep in the back of the car.

Gordon woke to Steve Miller's "Abracadabra" by The Steve Miller Band. It took him a moment to realize where he was and another long moment to remember why he was in the backseat of Simeon Kulak's Nova. The car was already moving. Gordon sat up just enough to see out the side window and saw only dark forest sliding by in a blur. They were already far from the party and passing through the wooded section of Fabers Road.

He had missed his opportunity.

Although it was too late to pull the prank in front of his classmates, Gordon thought he could still have a good story to tell if he gave Simpleton a little scare. The two of them would then laugh it off, and they could both joke about it at school on Monday, where everyone would see that there were no hard feelings about what had happened at the party.

Gordon made a low, growling sound and waited. The music continued to play on the radio, so he repeated the sound, only louder this time.

The car began to accelerate.

Gordon sat up in the back seat with his hands raised and fingers curled like claws. The mask jiggled and slipped down on his face, leaving him temporarily blinded as the eyeholes shifted downward. Simeon screamed, much louder than Gordon expected, and he quickly readjusted the mask so he could see again. He found Simeon turned the wrong way in the driver's seat, a look of pure terror on his face. Through the windshield, Gordon saw the car drift off the road and into the lot of Foreman's Garage. Gordon wanted to call out a warning, but was seized with panic when he realized they were about to crash into the flatbed truck parked in the lot.

Gordon dropped down onto the floor of the back seat just before the top of the car was sheared off.

36

Gordon slowly opened his eyes but was unable to immediately identify his surroundings. Wherever he was, it was very dark.

Had that been a dream?

It felt so real, as if it had happened just the night before, yet he was not in his bed or in the house where he grew up. Gordon closed his eyes. He remembered waking up the morning after the accident that ended Simeon Kulak's life, but it seemed like it had happened a very long time ago. He remembered walking home after the crash and realizing how lucky he was to have survived. Had he not ducked down in the backseat, he would have ended up just like Simeon.

Simpleton.

Gordon had not walked away from the crash unscathed. He had several bruises, and a piece of jagged metal had sliced through his shirt, cutting his back as he climbed out of the wreckage. He looked back at the car once he was out of it, the streetlamp illuminating the scene with its impassive glow. The front end of the Nova was crumpled under the rear of the truck, the roof peeled back like a half-opened sardine can. The back edge of the flatbed was touching the driver's seat headrest. Although he couldn't see it, he knew Simeon's body was under there somewhere. The shattered remains of the windshield lay strewn across the flatbed's deck plate, and at the far end, behind the cab and next to the winch, lay Simeon Kulak's severed head.

Gordon's eyes shot open. He had spent a lifetime trying to forget that image. He attempted to dispel the memory from his mind by focusing on his current situation and tried to sit up.

Nothing happened.

Confusion turned to panic as Gordon tried, and failed, to move any part of his body. He groaned loudly and felt an odd pain in his throat.

It was the only thing he felt.

He looked up toward the only source of light penetrating the gloom, realizing in that instant that he could move his eyes. A rectangular shaft of light shone down a flight of wooden stairs, and Gordon realized all at once where he was and how he had come to be there.

I'm in Uncle Milton's cellar, and he's...

Gordon turned his eyes in the opposite direction and gazed up at Uncle Milton's partially eaten face. The part of Gordon's brain responsible for motor skills sent frantic messages to other areas of his mind as it desperately struggled to animate his body. The realization that he was completely paralyzed fully set in, and the sense of panic became all-consuming. He began to hyperventilate, but he couldn't seem to draw enough air into his lungs. It felt as though his windpipe was obstructed or somehow constricted. Gordon turned his eyes away from his uncle's face and detected movement close by.

A rat emerged from a hole beneath the bottommost step, mere inches from his face, its whiskers twitching curiously. Despite his panicked state, he heard the voice of reason speak up for the last time.

So that's what lives behind the little door under the stairs.

The thought came and went in the chaos of Gordon's mind. Madness reigned as he watched the rat crawl out of the hole and onto his chest. Breathing became difficult, and then impossible.

37

Trey poured dry cat food into two of the three metal bowls on the back stoop of his mother's house, and cats streamed into the yard from multiple directions, drawn by the tinkling sound like hungry children to a dinner bell. The strays waited at a safe distance, still not entirely comfortable around their new caretaker. Trey tapped the ice out of the third bowl and then filled it with water from a plastic bottle.

"Come and get it!" he said to the half-dozen cats watching him.

The largest cat, a white one, strode forward, and the others followed at a close distance. Trey noticed dark stains on the cat's fur, mostly around its mouth but also on its chest. He had found a dead rat at the foot of the steps when he first walked around to the back of the house and thought the bloodstains—if that's what they were—identified the white guy as the one responsible for the rodent's demise.

Trey walked over to the fence to give the cats some space. They ascended the steps, but some had to wait for their superiors to take their share first. Looking down the neighboring driveway, Trey saw that the

Cadillac Gordon Nagel had been using recently was parked there, its windshield covered with a thin layer of frost. He hadn't seen Gordon during his last couple of visits to the house, and the car did not appear to have moved in a while, which struck him as unusual. Trey regularly drove past his mother's home while on the job and noticed that Milton Nagel's nephew frequently came and went since moving in next door. He was used to seeing the Cadillac at its usual spots around town: the 7-11, the local liquor store, and most often, the parking lot of Cormack's bar, but lately, he had only seen it in the driveway.

Looking at the back of Milton Nagel's house, Trey noticed that one of the windows was wide open. It was far too cold to justify an open window, which further piqued his curiosity about his mother's neighbor. He walked around the fence and past the car in the driveway. He looked at the front of the house and noticed that one of the front windows was also partially open. Something felt off, and Trey decided a friendly checkup was in order. He ascended the steps to the front porch and heard the television through the open window. He rang the doorbell and then knocked when no one answered. He stepped over to the window to look inside. The window curtains, partially drawn to the sides, swayed in the draft moving through the house. The window was open only a few inches, but Trey thought it was enough for him to be heard inside. The sill was low, at waist height, so he bent down and announced himself through the gap.

"Hello," he said. "Is anybody home? It's Trey Booker. Shirley's son."

He received no response, but he did detect an unpleasant odor emanating from inside the house. The smell reminded him of a recent house call that he and another officer had recently responded to. No one had answered the door at that residence either, and when the homeowner's daughter let them in, they found the resident dead in his recliner. The man had been dead for several days, and the house had reeked of death. It was an odor that Trey would not soon forget.

Blocking the outside light by cupping his hands against the glass, Trey scanned the interior once more. The place was a mess. The coffee table was cluttered with beer cans and discarded food packaging. Various items were scattered across the floor, yet he didn't notice anything—or anyone—that could account for the unmistakable smell of decay. He knocked on the glass and announced himself once again, but the only sound from inside came from the TV. He couldn't see the screen from where he stood, but the program playing sounded as if it were intended for children.

Trey weighed his options. He sensed something was wrong and realized that the only way to know for sure was to go inside. If he called the station, one or more of his fellow officers would be dispatched, but protocol would not permit them to take any further action beyond what he had already done. Only a family member could give them permission to enter the house, and Trey was only aware of his nephew, Gordon, whose car was parked in the driveway. He recalled Gordon telling him that his old clunker was in the shop when Trey had caught him drinking in the park the week before, and he had no reason to believe anything had changed since then, which implied that both men should be inside the house. If he was correct about the smell, at least one of them was dead.

Trey tested the doorknob and was surprised to find the door unlocked. Despite his reservations, he turned the knob and pushed it open. The foul smell struck him hard as he stepped inside, and he immediately pulled the collar of his shirt up over his nose. The indoor temperature felt even cooler than the outside. After a brief glance up the stairs, Trey moved toward the back of the house, stepping around discarded beer cans and an empty bottle of bleach. The rotting smell grew stronger as he entered the kitchen, which was in worse shape than the living room. One of the chairs lay on its side beside the kitchen table, and Trey noticed several other items scattered on the floor. There was a hammer, a tire iron, several bent nails, and what appeared to be a bundle of partially burned herbs. Beige-colored globs of hardened foam were plainly visible under the cabinets and in several parts of the kitchen. An uncapped, half-empty bottle of bourbon sat on the table. Crumpled beer cans were scattered on the counter, along with other miscellaneous garbage. The door next to the refrigerator stood half-open, with strips of duct tape clinging to its edges and a towel bunched up at the bottom. The layout of the house was identical to his mother's, so Trey knew the door led to the cellar. The kitchen's overhead light penetrated the darkness enough to illuminate the first few steps and the nearest part of the wall where the light switch and some scribbled numbers were located. Trey flipped the switch and gasped.

He had found the source of the stench.

Two bodies lay at the foot of the cellar stairs. Though barely recognizable in its current state, Trey knew that the one sitting with its back to the wall was what remained of Milton Nagel. He had clearly been dead for quite a while, but the condition of the body exceeded natural decomposition. Something had been consuming the remains, and Trey suspected rodents were the culprits. Most of the flesh had been stripped from the face. The eyes, lids, and surrounding tissue were entirely absent. The lower half of one ear was missing, while the other appeared to have been left untouched by the feeding creatures. Little remained of the nose. The lack of lips left the upper teeth visible, and the jaw hung wide open, revealing the black gunk that must once have been a tongue. A sweater mottled with what might be bleach stains hung loosely from Milton Nagel's shoulders.

Gordon Nagel lay with his head in his dead uncle's

lap. His eyes were still intact, suggesting he had not been dead long enough to entice the scavengers. Although his lifeless gaze was generally directed upward at Milton, his head appeared to be turned slightly too far in relation to the position of his shoulders. One arm lay beneath his body, while the other rested beside him. One of his legs was partially entangled in a collapsed wheelchair that lay to the side of the stairs.

Trey desperately needed air. He had been holding his breath with one hand covering his mouth and pinching his nostrils, but he didn't want to inhale any more of the foul air that permeated the house. He bolted for the front door, gasping as he burst out onto the front porch. He felt lightheaded and sat down on the front steps next to the wheelchair ramp, where he took several controlled breaths. A woman strolled along the sidewalk across the street with a young girl skipping at her heels.

"Merry Christmas!" the little girl shouted, waving at Trey.

Trey returned the wave, and the innocence of the moment helped to calm his nerves. He took out his phone and called headquarters.

38

Trey pushed the wheelchair up the ramp, then turned his mother around on the front porch. They both saw Detective Soto pull up next door as Trey backed into the house through the front door.

"Now what?" Shirley asked her son. "I thought they were all done with everything over there."

"I don't know," Trey said, parking the wheelchair beside the sofa and engaging the brake. "Let me help you up."

Shirley extended her arm, and Trey helped his mother to stand. He positioned the walker in front of her, and she shifted her weight onto the handles.

"I just want to forget about what went on in that house," she said, sounding slightly winded from the effort of standing, "but how can I with police detectives comin' and goin' all the time?"

"I know, Mama. He's probably just wrapping things up."

"You said that the last time your detective friend showed up," Shirley said, moving slowly toward the bathroom.

"I'll go talk to him. Do you need help in there?"

"I'll be fine. I still have some pride left. Just bring in the flowers from Mazie when you come back inside. I want to put them in a vase."

Trey waited until his mother closed the bathroom door before going outside. The sun was high in the sky, and the day was already unseasonably warm. Detective Soto stood on the front porch of Milton Nagel's house, a bunched-up wad of police tape in one hand. Trey's eyes were drawn to the second floor when he thought he saw movement behind one of the upstairs windows.

"Hey, Trey," Soto said, descending the front steps.

"Hey, Victor," Trey returned. "Are we no longer living next to a crime scene?"

"I guess you could say that."

Trey looked again at the upstairs window. "Is someone here with you?"

The detective turned to follow Trey's gaze. "No, just me. Why?"

Trey shook his head. "Just wondering," he said, accepting that he had been mistaken about seeing something at the window.

"How's that ramp working out for you?"

Trey glanced over his shoulder at the wheelchair ramp that Milton Nagel's niece, Karen, had gifted to his mother. "It's great," he said. "It was sure nice of her to offer it."

"Ah, it was no use to her anyway. How's your mother doing?"

"A little better every day. I just worry about her falling. She tries to do too much, and she's impossibly stubborn."

Detective Soto offered an understanding nod and then turned back to look up at the Nagel residence. "The old place will be up for sale soon," he said. "Karen Williams said it'll be priced to sell. Said she won't be able to get rid of it soon enough." He gave Trey a sideways glance. "Maybe you should buy it. Move in next door to your mom."

"That's a hard pass," said Trey. "I'd never be able to live in there after seeing what I saw in the cellar."

"Yeah, I won't be forgetting that any time soon either."

The image of the two dead men resurfaced in Trey's mind, and he blinked hard, hoping to erase it. He pointed his chin at the wadded police tape in the detective's hand. "So, is the case officially closed now?"

"That's up to the DA," Soto said with a shrug. "But I assume he'll want to. I summarized my assessment in the report, and I'm pretty sure I got it right. Most of it, anyway. Besides, there's no one alive to charge with anything."

"So, what exactly do you think happened?" Trey asked. "How long had they been dead?"

"The medical examiner said the younger one, Gordon Nagel, had only been dead for a day or two. He estimated that the old man had been dead for at least a week, maybe longer, but couldn't say for sure due to the decomposition of the body and the damage the rats had done."

Trey nodded, crinkling his nose at the realization that his assumption about the rats had been accurate.

The detective nodded when he noticed Trey's reaction. "Yeah," he said, "the house is infested with them. Especially the cellar. Found a huge nest in the storage space under the stairs. The food source was right there for them. Someone sprayed foam sealer throughout the house, around the radiator pipes, along the floorboards, and in any space where a rat might squeeze through. Whichever one of them did it made a hell of a mess. It looked like shit, but I think he managed to confine the rats to the cellar."

Trey grimaced as the haunting image of the dead men returned, only this time with rats feasting on flesh. "So, Milton had been dead for at least a week while Gordon was living in the house?"

"That's right."

"And do you still think Gordon killed him?" Trey asked, recalling what the detective had told him the last time they spoke.

"Yep. I'm sure of it."

Trey encouraged him to elaborate by raising his

eyebrows.

"The old man's death was no accident. A wheelchair, specifically the one we found in the cellar, could not fit through the door at the top of the stairs, so he didn't roll through it by accident. Someone had to fold it up and throw it down there afterward. Gordon Nagel either killed his uncle first and then left the body in the cellar, or threw him down there and waited for him to die."

Trey turned to the detective, unable to disguise the look of shock on his face. "You think he locked him down there while he was still alive?"

"Hard to say for sure, but there's reason to believe he was alive down there for at least a little while."

Trey couldn't form another question. He just stared at the house as Detective Soto laid out his hypothesis.

"Milton Nagel was found sitting with his back to the wall. It's virtually impossible—and the ME agreed—that the body would have ended up that way after falling down the stairs. It stands to reason that he maneuvered himself into that position on his own."

"So he *was* alive," Trey muttered, half to himself.

"It appears so. For how long, though, we can't say for sure. It's possible that the nephew pushed him down the stairs, hoping to kill him that way, but it's also possible that he did something beforehand. The autopsy found a small fracture on the old man's skull, and there were signs of a contusion on the skin in that area. The presence of a bruise indicates that he was alive for some length of time after sustaining the injury."

"So, you think Gordon may have hit him with something before throwing him in the cellar?"

The detective nodded. "That's what I think happened. Maybe he thought he was dead at first, but I'm convinced he knew he was still alive down there."

"How's that?"

"Because the door had been nailed shut. Why would he do that if he didn't believe his uncle might try to get out? He must have known he was still alive."

Trey recalled seeing the hammer and nails on the kitchen floor. "And the duct tape," he said, remembering that as well.

"Yeah," Detective Soto said, nodding. "He taped up the seams around the door, too, but that was probably because of the smell. He just left him to rot down there. For at least a week. The place stunk to high hell."

Trey cringed, recalling the dreadful smell that had greeted him when he had gone inside. "Why did he stick around? You'd think he would have hightailed it out of town after that."

"I think he wanted to, but he was trying to accumulate enough money first. I interviewed several people who knew him, including you, of course, and everything points in that direction."

"I'm listening," Trey prompted.

"I interviewed the bartender who works at Cormack's, where Gordon Nagel was a regular. He said Nagel had been asking questions about how power of attorney and joint bank accounts operated, and Mack, the bartender, said he'd asked in a way that made him suspicious of his motives. Said he even warned him not to do anything stupid. I learned some other pertinent things from Mack the Bartender, but I'll stay on point.

"I followed up at the bank and checked Nagel's bank records. Gordon Nagel was granted POA at the end of November. His sister, Karen, the one who gave you the wheelchair ramp, had flown in to help set it up with a lawyer. When I interviewed her, she said that her brother was not good with finances or responsibility in general, but convinced Milton Nagel to agree to it since Karen lives in Colorado and would not be immediately available in case of an emergency. Milton had recently had an accident where he broke both his ankles, and he wasn't showing much improvement, so that was the motivation. They also added Gordon's name to Milton's bank account in case he needed access to money in an emergency. Nothing unusual happened with the account until the eleventh of December, when Gordon Nagel requested an ATM card for it. He withdrew money that day and nearly every day afterward up until the twenty-first."

"Do you think that's when Gordon died?"

"Most likely. You found him dead two days later, on the twenty-third."

"Do you think he was taking money out a little at a time until he had enough to skip town?"

"No, there wasn't that much in the account. He probably spent most of that money on booze. You saw all those empty liquor bottles and beer cans, right?"

Trey nodded.

"Milton Nagel received a pension deposit at the beginning of every month. I think Gordon was waiting for that."

"I guess that makes sense," said Trey. "So, if Gordon started withdrawing money after his uncle's death, then that corroborates the examiner's estimate."

"Yep."

"I just don't see how Gordon could have put up with that smell for all that time."

"Oh, he tried to cover it up," the detective said, shaking his head. "Did you notice those bleach bottles when you were inside?"

Trey recalled seeing at least one bottle of bleach on the living room floor and nodded.

"The fucking guy drilled a hole through the floor and poured bleach into the cellar. Can you believe it?"

"I didn't smell bleach when I was in there," said Trey.

"Because it doesn't last that long. It might cover up the smell for a little while, but it certainly won't eliminate it. He made the hole close to the place where the body was down below. Maybe he thought it would work if he drenched the corpse in it."

"Did he?"

"What? Drench the corpse?" The detective shook his head. "No, the hole was off the mark, and most of the liquid ended up on the floor between the dead guy's legs. Some of it splashed onto his clothes, but that's about it. I think that proves he was afraid to go into the cellar to address the problem directly."

"But how did Gordon end up in the cellar?" Trey asked. "Why did he open the door?"

"The furnace seized up and shut down at some point, though there's no way to know exactly when. Maybe he was going down there to check it out and fell down the stairs. He was probably drunk out of his mind."

Trey recalled the open windows and how cold the house had been when he was inside and reasoned that the furnace might have overheated and shut down while trying to maintain the temperature.

"There was a bundle of burnt herbs on the kitchen floor," Detective Soto continued. "He was probably carrying that with him to help him deal with the smell down there. The fact that it was found upstairs by the door implies that he'd dropped it before falling from the top. Broke his neck on the way down."

"Is that the official cause of death?" Trey asked. "A broken neck?"

"Yes, but the ME said he probably didn't die right away. Said he may have lain there for a while before suffocating."

"Suffocating?"

"Yeah, he said it had something to do with the way his neck was broken. It slowly constricts the airway in the windpipe. It doesn't really matter, though."

Trey imagined what Gordon Nagel's last moments must have been like, gazing up at that rotting corpse, his head cradled in his uncle's lap.

"Wanna know the most fucked up thing about all this?" the detective said, turning to face Trey. "There was enough cash in that house for Gordon Naleg to have walked away rich."

"How's that?"

"There was a safe inside a little closet under the cellar stairs. The closet was padlocked, but we found the key in one of the kitchen drawers. We couldn't open the safe until we obtained permission from Karen Williams, but when we did, we found fifty thousand in cash, a collection of old coins, and some gold bars. Probably around a hundred grand in all."

"Holy crap!" Trey exclaimed. "Did you have to bust it open?"

"No, we didn't," Soto said, smiling broadly. "The safe had a combination lock on it. We asked Karen if she knew the combination, but she didn't even know about the safe. With her permission, we searched the house for anything with numbers written on it, and one of the guys spotted the combination in plain sight."

"Where was that?" Trey asked.

"On the wall above the cellar light switch."

"You're kidding."

Detective Soto chuckled softly. "Gordon Nagel had been sitting on top of a pile of money the whole time, and he could have easily accessed it if only he had looked. And the thing is, he would have inherited half of that money and the house if he'd just waited for his uncle to die naturally."

"So why did he kill him then? What was his motive?"

"That's something we'll probably never know. The guy was a raging alcoholic, which opens doors to many possibilities, none of them good. It may have been nothing more than an argument that got out of hand."

Trey recalled the day he found Gordon Nagel drunk in the park, and wondered how it fit into Soto's proposed timeline. He thought he had been doing Gordon a favor by letting him walk to his uncle's house. He hoped he wasn't wrong.

"Well, I'm clocking out for the day," Detective Soto said, interrupting Trey's thoughts. "Feel like joining me for a drink?"

Trey had never been much of a drinker, and he certainly didn't want one now. He cast a final glance at the Nagel house and then turned to face the detective. "No thanks," he said. "I gotta take care of my mom."

Trey retrieved the flowers Mazie had given his mother from the car and held them under his nose. He closed his eyes and inhaled the fragrant scent, but it only brought to mind the smell he wished he could forget. Still, he held the flowers close under his chin as he climbed the stairs to his mother's front door.

ACKNOWLEDGEMENT

Thank you for reading, and thank you in advance for leaving a rating and/or review, should you be so inclined. Nothing is more helpful to a writer.

I leave it to you to decide what really happened inside Uncle Milton's house. Was Gordon haunted by a ghost or a guilty conscience? Or maybe both? You can draw your own conclusions on that matter, but ultimately, it was Gordon's addiction that led to his downfall.

I have lost some very close friends to addiction, but I am proud to know others who are winning the fight against that demon every day. I'm no expert, so I won't offer advice on alcoholism or other addictions, but I do know help is available if you need it.

Thank you, Vonnie Mott, Cindy Scalera, and Rob Malave for reading early drafts of this book and providing feedback. Most of all, I want to thank my wife, Lizzy, for supporting my writing and all my other pursuits in life. I couldn't do it without you.

J.J. Mott

ABOUT THE AUTHOR

J. J. Mott

J.J. Mott is a musician and instructor
who dedicates much of his
remaining time to writing. He finds
reality terrifying enough, so he
creates fictional stories where he
and his readers can escape to a more
palatable dreadfulness.

J.J. (Jeff) lives in New Jersey with his wife, dogs,
and various other critters. He grows hot peppers for
homemade hot sauce and other fiery concoctions.

BOOKS BY THIS AUTHOR

Deadly Miracle

Two men rob a convenience store during a winter storm, only to veer off the road during their escape. Separated during the accident, each is unaware that the other survived.

  Teenager Faye McKenna broods in her room a short distance from the scene of the accident, wishing for an escape from her miserable life with her stepfather and his cold-hearted mother.

  The accident survivors find their way to Faye's house and discover something entirely unexpected inside.

The Thing That Calls

12 Tales of Horror and Suspense. Volume 1

The Thing That Calls 2

12 Tales of Horror and Suspense. Volume 2

www.ingramcontent.com/pod-product-compliance
Lightning Source LLC
Chambersburg PA
CBHW060628260626
47161CB00008B/2832